The Swing

Bradbury Press   Scarsdale, New York

The Swing

BY EMILY HANLON

Thanks to Beth Maley, a teacher of deaf children, who read my manuscript and answered my questions.—E.H.

5 4 3 2 1   79 80 81 82 83
The text of this book is set in 12 pt. Baskerville.

Library of Congress Cataloging in Publication Data
    Hanlon, Emily. The swing
Summary: An 11-year-old deaf girl and a 13-year-old boy with family problems seek refuge at a swing which has come to have a special meaning for each of them.
    [1. Friendship—Fiction]   I. Title.
PZ7.H1964Sw   [Fic]   78-26400
ISBN 0-87888-146-8

The Swing

For Natasha, who has loved this book for a very
   long time;
For Nicky, who, like Beth, would see the beauty
   of the bears; and
For Dick, whose guidance and inspiration are so
   much a part of *The Swing*.

~ I ~
Across the Field

Chapter One

As soon as Beth felt the car stop, she opened the door, jumped out and began running. Her mother's hand brushed across her shoulder to stop her. Beth pretended not to feel it. She knew what her mother wanted. She wanted Beth to help unpack. But Beth had all summer to unpack. Now she had something more important to do—something she'd been waiting for since they'd closed up the cottage last September. She had to run through the field and yell and shout and laugh as loudly as she could. Then she had to go for a ride on the swing.

So Beth pretended not to feel her mother's hand. There was no other way for Mrs. Hampton to stop Beth unless she ran after her. She couldn't yell for her to stop because Beth was deaf.

At the end of the driveway, Beth paused and looked back over her shoulder. Her mother and father were already busy unloading the car. *Good, they've forgotten about me!* She plunged into the tall thick grass growing in the field.

A cool evening breeze was blowing. Beth thought of the long, hot, boring hours she'd spent in the car that day—but now that she was here, it didn't matter. She took a deep breath. The air smelled wonderful, better than she remembered. Wildflowers were everywhere. Stopping to pick a few, she began running through the field. She caught her pants on some prickles and fell, rolling in the grass, shouting and laughing.

If somebody heard her they might think she was in trouble or frightened—her voice was low, as if the sounds were coming from deep down inside her body, and to some people it seemed as though Beth spoke with a foreign accent. Others found her speaking difficult to understand. But in the field she could laugh and shout and there was nobody to listen to her, nobody to tell her to talk more slowly the way her mother always did—it didn't matter what she sounded like here.

Beth stood up. There was something different about the field this year, but she couldn't figure out what. Turning around and around, she looked in all directions. She knelt down and pulled at the grass and smelled it. When she stood again, she knew what it was.

It's the grass! she thought. *I can see above the tall grass!*

For the first time in her life Beth was taller than the grass in the field—without standing on her toes. It made her feel silly and happy and she began to run again, tearing at the grass, throwing it up in the air and laughing as the pieces floated down on her.

So I am growing, she thought. Everyone had told her she was; but she hadn't believed them. This was different. The grass was positive, scientific proof she was growing.

Beth was eleven in May, but a small eleven. The smallest eleven she knew anyway. "Petite" was the way her mother put it. Beth didn't like that word much: "petite." It was too fancy. There was nothing wrong with being plain small. Small and quick and alert like the animals in the field—rabbits, chipmunks and field mice—small and quiet, running in and out of the tall grass, forever free and happy. And even the deer—they weren't so little, but they weren't so big either—just fast and graceful. Every summer morning Beth could see the deer from her window as they came down the mountain, circled around the outskirts of town, through the field and around behind the cottage to the woods. Beth knew their trail. Sometimes she followed it and sat watching the deer . . . beautiful, silent creatures.

The brambles in the field were getting thicker now. Tangled vines seemed to be strangling it like hungry sea monsters with thousands of long tentacles. Beth looked around for the trail where the vines would be trampled down by the deer as they made their daily journey through the field and past her swing.

Her swing! The thought of it tickled something inside her and she laughed out loud. Her swing. The most wonderful swing in the world!

It wasn't exactly her swing. Nobody had bought it for her. Nobody had given it to her. Her father hadn't put it up, and it wasn't on their property. It hung from a long branch on the old oak tree at the other end of the field, almost halfway between her house and the Gradys'. Beth didn't think the swing belonged to the Gradys because if it did, Danny Grady probably would have made her ask permission to use it. He was two years older than Beth and always hanging around with Willy Donaldson and Brian Stone. The three of them acted like big shots when they were together, showing off and pushing each other about all the time. They didn't bother with Beth too much except for Willy. Sometimes, when she was in town, he'd sneak up on her to scare her, or imitate the way she spoke. Sometimes it made her mad and sometimes she ignored it.

Danny was the only other person Beth had ever seen on the swing. She didn't like the idea of having to share the swing with him. She didn't like the idea of Danny having the swing all to himself during the winter. The swing belonged to her—to her and the old oak.

~

Once Beth found the deer trail, she ran quickly without tripping until she saw the ropes of the swing hanging from the big old branch. She stopped and sighed in relief—she was never sure when she came back after the winter whether the swing would still be there. It might blow down in a storm. Even the old oak could fall. It was very old.

Beth began to run again, breaking out of the

tall grass and across the field of dandelions, running so fast she could only stop by crashing into the trunk of the oak. She leaned against it, breathless, and hugged it, feeling warm and happy inside.

"Hello, Mr. Oak," she said out loud, and giggled. She never thought of talking to any other tree, but there was something about the oak that held her swing—something special and private, something she couldn't explain, something she felt. Maybe it was the way it stood, tall and straight and silent, looking over the valley—old and wise, knowing so many things, and keeping them all a secret.

"Hello, Mr. Oak," Beth began again. "I missed you, Sir Oak. I hope you had a good winter. I hope it wasn't too cold. And I hope you didn't lose any important branches to a storm. And especially I hope you took good care of my swing!"

She patted the oak and laughed. "I'm glad you're still here!" she shouted, and jumped on the swing.

The oak grew on top of a small hill overlooking the center of Chester Falls and the countryside beyond. It wasn't a very big hill—*just big enough to see what you want to see,* Beth thought. From the swing the view was even better. Back and forth and back and forth: the small buildings of Chester Falls, Main Street, and the checkered farm land mixing and swaying like colors in a kaleidoscope. The faster Beth pumped, the crazier the picture became: the white church steeple mixing with the big bright-red barns of Mr. Clarke's dairy farm, mixing with the green pastures and the newly tilled brown farming land. White and red, brown and green. Back and forth. Up and down. Woosh! The colors mixing and blending with the pink-streaked sky and the green and gray cliffs and peaks of Mt. Ash.

Higher and higher, faster and faster Beth flew, laughing and shouting. "Hello, Chester Falls! Hello, Mt. Ash! Hello, Mr. and Mrs. Clarke! Hello, Jamie Clarke! Hello! Hello! Hello! I'm back!" Beth shouted to everyone and everything she knew. She shouted to the Clarkes' cows. She shouted to Peggy Dwyer and to Mr. McGowan's dog, Buster, and to the two old ladies with white frizzy hair whom everyone called the Misses Dawson. She shouted to Mr. and Mrs. Willard, Mr. Sharpe, and Clem Cintron.

"This is the best day!" she shouted to the world. As she threw back her head and kicked her feet high into the air, a boy appeared at the edge of the field. He crouched in the tall grass, watching her.

Beth couldn't see the boy—she was pumping hard, swinging so fast, faster than she could ever remember swinging. When she closed her eyes it was almost like flying. Someday she might swing so hard and fly so far she would get tangled in the tallest branches of the old oak. Someday her father was going to build her a tree house in the oak. Someday she was going to spend the night in the mountains with him. Someday she was going to come to Chester Falls and never leave. Someday the cottage would be hers. Someday she was going to become a forest ranger and live in the mountains—maybe even here on Mt. Ash. There was an old fire tower on the top, and she could stay there because someday she was going to be in charge of the whole mountain! And tomorrow she was going to climb the mountain alone, without her father, without anyone, just as she'd been dreaming about for weeks.

Beth stopped pumping, and the swing came slowly to a stop. It was getting dark, and she knew she should leave. She didn't like walking through the field alone in the dark. The moon cast scary shadows on the tall grass, and it was easy to trip. But it was hard to leave the swing and the old oak now—it had been such a long time.

~

Danny hid in the tall grass, waiting for Beth to leave. *Why does she have to be here tonight of all nights?* he thought angrily. Then he shouted out loud, "Get out of here! Get out of here and leave me alone!"

Even though Beth couldn't hear him, the shouting made Danny feel better. It helped calm the rage that had sent him racing out of the house, away from his mother and Clyde, to the solitude of the swing. His swing. His place when he needed to be alone. *Typical of my luck she's here now,* he thought, angrily pulling at the grass. Nothing seemed to be going right lately. Sometimes he wondered if it ever would again.

When Beth finally left the swing, Danny hurried to it. But he didn't swing. He never used it for swinging anymore. Wrapping his arms around the ropes, he thought of when he was little and he came here with his father. Sometimes his father would push him and sometimes they would swing together, Danny sitting on his shoulders. Or they would play games around the oak tree: cowboys and Indians, pirates, hide-and-seek. No matter what game they played, the rock in front of the oak was always safety because Pterodactyl, the flying dinosaur, lived there. All Danny had to do then was touch the rock, and Pterodactyl would come to help him. Grasping the ropes tightly with his fingers, Danny leaned back and looked up into the huge leafy branches of the tree where he used to imagine Pterodactyl slept at night, keeping watch over the swing, the field, and even Danny.

Pterodactyl had begun when Danny and his father first turned over the rock in front of the oak tree, and found strange markings imprinted on the underside.

"It's most likely the fossil of some animal or plant," his father had said.

After examining it, Danny told his father, "I think it's a dinosaur's foot. I bet a dinosaur lived right here in the field."

His father had laughed. "Dinosaurs' feet were much bigger than that."

"Not flying dinosaurs," Danny had answered. And when they got home, they looked through Danny's dinosaur book and found a picture of Pterodactyl. It was hard to tell if his feet really looked anything like the markings on the rock, but that didn't change Danny's mind. To Danny and his father the markings were real dinosaur prints, and that made Pterodactyl real, too.

Danny got off the swing and walked to the rock. Kneeling down, he laid his hands on it. "Hey, Pterodactyl, you still there?" he whispered. "I sure could use some help now."

Almost in answer to Danny's question, Beth's loud grating laughter echoed across the field. She was calling for her father, shouting and laughing. The sound of her voice maddened Danny. She had had her turn at the swing. Now it was his turn, and he needed to be alone—alone with the silence of the place.

Chapter Two

"Daddy! Daddy!" Beth shouted excitedly.

Mr. Hampton was unloading the last of the boxes from the car. He turned to Beth and waved.

"I'm taller than the grass!" she shouted as she ran from the field.

"What?" Mr. Hampton asked as Beth crashed into him. "What?" he repeated when she looked up.

"I'm taller than the grass in the field," she said slowly and distinctly.

Her father laughed. "You see. I told you."

Beth giggled and threw her arms around her father. "I'm so happy we're back!"

"Well, tell me—is everything all right in the field? Is the swing still there?"

Beth felt herself blushing, and she laughed self-consciously. All her fears about something happening to the swing over the winter seemed silly now. "Yes," she said and quickly added, "can I help you unload?"

"I think this is the last of it."

"Is Mom mad because I didn't help?"

"A little, but she'll get over it. Besides, there's still plenty to do inside."

Beth helped her father carry in one of the boxes. Mrs. Hampton was in the kitchen, preparing dinner. She frowned when she saw Beth.

"Why did you run off like that?" she demanded.

"I'm sorry."

"You're always sorry afterward, Beth."

"Let her be," Mr. Hampton interrupted. "It was a long drive. She just needed to get out and run. Besides, she's promised she'll help now. Right, Beth?"

Beth nodded.

"Oh, all right," her mother sighed. "You can start by setting the table. But you'll have to rinse off the dishes first. They've been collecting dust all winter."

As Beth set the table, she began dreaming one of her favorite dreams—living in Chester Falls all year round. Without looking at anyone, she timidly suggested, "You know, there wouldn't be so much work to do when we came for the summer if the cottage wasn't closed up all winter." As soon as the words were out of her mouth, she glanced at her mother for the inevitable response.

"You're not going to start in on that again?" Mrs. Hampton said irritably.

"But I don't mean we should live here *all* winter. Just on vacations and times like that. Then the house wouldn't get so dusty. Or maybe we could come just on vacation. Oh, please. That would be so wonderful—to come here on Christmas!"

"You know perfectly well we can't live here in the winter," her mother sighed. "There's no heat. The pipes freeze. It's just not meant to be an all-year house."

"Other people live in Chester Falls in the winter," Beth insisted.

"And they have sturdy, winterized houses."

"Couldn't we do that to this house?"

"I suppose," her father said. "But it would take an awful lot of money."

"It could be my birthday and Christmas presents for ever and ever, Daddy."

Her father grinned. "Then I suppose you'd want to move up here for good."

Beth couldn't help smiling. That's what she wanted more than anything.

As Beth carried the dishes to the table, her mother stared hard at her as if she were annoyed by Beth's dreams. "And what would we do up here?" she demanded, handing her the glasses. "Where would your father work? Where would you go to school? Do you think they have schools for deaf children in places like Chester Falls? Do you think you'd ever have learned to talk so well if you lived here?"

Talking! Beth was sick of it. As if talking was the most important thing in the world—as if her talking was some kind of miracle. Her mother didn't understand. She never understood anything except that Beth should talk clearly so she could ask for help if she was lost, and that she could talk "pleasantly" so she didn't embarrass anybody. Beth knew her mother used to be embarrassed by the way she sounded. But now she was proud of Beth. The teacher had told her that Beth could be ready for a regular school in another year, if the Hamptons wanted. Beth definitely didn't want that.

Sometimes she wished she'd never learned to talk. Before she'd gone to school, she'd lived in a silent world where she, her mother and her father had learned to express themselves to each other in their own, special, quiet way. But when she went to school, Beth discovered she would have to learn to communicate with a world that wasn't quiet, a world where speaking and hearing were as important and natural as breathing.

At first Beth hated and resented the long, frustrating hours she had to spend learning how to form words she would never hear. Her teachers told her she was lucky because she could lip-read so easily, and although she knew it was true—there were still kids in her class who had trouble lipreading—it didn't seem to make speaking any easier. Sometimes Beth wondered if it was worth the effort.

And then, one day a couple of years ago, it all seemed to fall into place. She could feel herself forming the words; she could feel herself speaking, and she laughed out loud from happiness: she had learned to speak—the silent, lonely barrier separating her from the hearing world was about to crumble. At least she thought it was. But it didn't. Not completely. Hearing kids still stared at her when she spoke, as if she were a freak. Some kids still called her dummy. Strangers became flustered or embarrassed when they realized she was different, and sometimes they'd look away from her as if she didn't exist. Beth hated that most of all. Sometimes she felt like strangling the person, grabbing him and screaming, "Look at me. I'm no different from you. I can think! I can see! I can smell! And I feel all the things that you feel!"

Talking and learning and school—they didn't seem to matter much after all. That's why she liked coming to Chester Falls so much. There was something about the country—the field, the mountain, the swing, and the town—that made her forget about being deaf. Being different. Everyone in Chester Falls knew her, and most people liked her—except for kids like Willy Donaldson, but they didn't really matter. She knew when she went into town tomorrow people would be happy to see her.

"It's summer. I don't want to think about school," Beth said as they sat down to dinner.

"That's fair," her father agreed and then said, "If you had one wish for something special this summer, Beth—what would you wish?"

"Besides living here for the winter!" her mother teased.

Beth didn't think her mother was very funny. She thought about her wish for a moment and said, "That the swing was all mine and Danny Grady never used it."

"That's a silly wish," her mother said. "The swing is for everyone."

"Maybe, but lots of times when I want to go swinging—he's there. Just sitting. Sitting. It's not fair. A swing is for swinging—not sitting!"

"It's for anything a person wants it to be," her mother added. "I don't know why you have to be like that about Danny. He's always seemed like a nice boy."

"Danny? Ugh!" Beth frowned.

"You and Danny used to play together," her mother went on.

"Never!" Beth insisted as she picked the onions and peppers out of the salad, pushing them off her plate.

Mrs. Hampton grabbed her hand. "Don't do that."

"I hate onions and peppers!"

"Then just leave them on your plate."

"But the onions smell."

"Beth," her mother sighed impatiently.

Mr. Hampton reached across the table and touched Beth to get her attention. "You did play with Danny, you know. Before his father died. You must have been five or six. Andy, that was his father, was very fond of you. Every night after dinner he and Danny would take you for a walk in the field. Don't you remember that at all?"

Beth thought for a moment and memories of Danny's father began returning, vague at first; then in a flash, she saw him pushing her on the swing at dusk. Danny was there, too, standing over her on the swing, twisting and pulling at the ropes, making the swing zigzag. . . . It was funny, very funny, and Danny's father was laughing, too. And then another memory of Danny's father: she was alone with him on the back porch, blowing very hard on a long wooden flute. He was nodding his head in approval, smiling, clapping his hands together. As she blew harder and harder, the vibrations of the flute tickled her tongue, and she laughed out loud. Again and again she blew on the flute until she was filled with the sensation of the flute's music.

Beth could hear many sounds clearly with her hearing aid; but the flute wasn't one of them. The flute was more of a feeling and she could only imagine the music it made. She knew for sure it wasn't anything like the drums, which was one of the first sounds her teachers had taught her to distinguish. Drum sounds were easy, like the crashing of the subway, the rumble of traffic in the city, or the roar of a lion she had once heard in the zoo. She could hear cars honking, doors slamming, and sometimes even people shouting; but the closest she'd come to hearing soft, gentle sounds were the times she'd played the flute herself.

Now as she sat remembering the flute, the way it felt, and how much she'd loved to play it, she felt herself smiling. The flute was such a nice memory—she wondered why she didn't think about it more often. . . .

When she looked up at her parents, they were still talking about Danny's father. She wanted to ask them about the flute; but she felt silly. Maybe she wasn't remembering right. Why would anyone give her a flute? Instead she said, "I think I do remember Danny's father."

Her mother smiled. "He was such a friendly man. . . ." And then she shook her head. "It was a shame he died—a car accident . . ."

But Beth wasn't listening to her mother's recollections. She was thinking about the flute.

~

When her father came to kiss her good night, Beth pulled him close and asked, "Daddy, did I ever have a flute?"

"A flute? Why?"

"Because—I remember something. But it's silly. Why would I have a flute?"

"Wait a minute. You did have a flute. Danny's father made you one. It must have been our talking about him that made you remember."

Beth nodded and her father went on. "It was the summer just before he died. He'd carved a flute out of wood for Danny. When you saw it, you were fascinated. You blew on it and blew on it until you were all red in the face." He laughed.

"I don't think that's so funny. I remembered it all tonight—even how it felt."

"I'm sorry, sweetheart," her father apologized. "I didn't mean to laugh at you. I was just remembering how you looked that first time. It was wonderful, though. You used to say it tickled your tongue. And when you blew very hard, you thought you could hear something. When you told Andy that, he was determined to teach you how to play. He spent hours showing you how to blow on it gently, and after a while, you actually didn't sound too bad! You loved that flute so much, you carried it with you wherever you went that summer."

"What happened to it?"

"It got lost, I suppose. The way toys do . . ."

Beth felt sad. "I wish I hadn't lost it. How many deaf kids have someone make a flute for them?"

Her father leaned over and kissed her. "Well, you still have the memory."

Reaching up, Beth threw her arms around his neck, and holding him very tightly she exclaimed, "This really is the best place in the whole world, Daddy!"

Chapter Three

Danny knelt by the rock, slowly and gently rubbing his fingers back and forth across its smooth surface. Maybe if he stayed here long enough, his mother and Clyde would go to bed.

No. Clyde'll wait. He'll wait all night if he has to, and Ma will wait because Clyde's waiting. . . .

"Danny! Are you out there?" Mrs. Grady's voice cut through the silence.

"I'm coming," Danny shouted. He didn't want anyone to find him here.

His mother was looking for him where the lawn turned into the field. "Danny, you better come in and talk to him. You shouldn't have run off like that."

"I'm not gonna help him. That's all."

"I know it's hard. I know you don't like it, but Clyde's been good to you. He needs you tomorrow with that cow. He knows you don't like slaughtering. That's why he never asks you. But tomorrow is different. Strangs' cow has a broken leg, and it can't be fixed," she said, reaching out for Danny, grabbing his hand apologetically.

Danny pulled away. "Yeah, well, I'm not helping, Ma."

"You have to talk to him, Danny. Now Clyde's been real good to you."

Danny laughed bitterly. "I'm sick of you telling me that. You think telling me that all the time is gonna make it so?"

"Don't say things like that. . . ."

The screen door opened.

"Danny, that you out there?" Clyde called impatiently.

"Yeah."

'I want you to come inside. We got to talk now."

"I'm coming."

As Danny followed Clyde into the kitchen, the smell of the smokehouse that surrounded Clyde wherever he went filled Danny's nostrils. He hated the smokehouse. He hated the fact that his mother had worked there since she'd married Clyde, taking orders and selling the bacon, sausages and hams from the front of the store. But most of all he hated the butchering. He'd seen hogs slaughtered only twice, and that was enough. Both times he'd watched in horror as one of the men had held the squealing hog, and Clyde quickly slit its throat with an easy flick of his wrist.

It took a minute for Danny to adjust his eyes to the bright kitchen light. "Sit down, now," Clyde said abruptly and when Danny was seated, he went on. "So you have no stomach for slaughtering, huh?"

Danny didn't answer. He glanced at his mother. She looked tired in the ugly glare of the kitchen light. A moth flew in front of her, and she brushed it aside.

Clyde waited for Danny to answer, but when it was clear he wasn't going to, Clyde shook his head and sighed despairingly. "You know, I don't understand you, Danny. Why if I was you, I'd at least be interested in finding out about a business that was gonna be mine someday. Here I am, not even your blood father, and I'm setting up a business for you to just walk into." He paused for a moment, drawing deeply on his cigar before going on. "I'm sorry you don't like the slaughtering, but it's a part of the business. It ain't the best part to be sure, but there's a lot of other jobs far worse, boy —let me tell you."

Danny continued staring at the table. *I can't hear you, Clyde. I'm not even listening,* he thought. *You can keep on talking all you want, but I'm not gonna answer you, Clyde. You don't even exist.*

"Look at me, boy, when I'm talking to you!" Clyde demanded.

For a second their eyes met. *I'm not giving in,* Danny told Clyde in his head. *There's nothing you can do to make me slaughter that cow. Nothing.* But he didn't speak to Clyde; instead he looked deliberately away, a weary, bored expression on his face.

"Well, like it or not, you're gonna start learning the business, boy, because I need your help." Clyde chewed impatiently on his cigar, waiting for Danny to respond. "What's the matter with you?" he suddenly shouted. "You too fancy to get blood on you?"

"Calm down, Clyde," Mrs. Grady interrupted; and turning to Danny she said, "Your father's making a lot of sense. It's time you showed some interest in the smokehouse, Danny."

Danny turned from her, too. *He's not my father! He's never gonna be my father! Why did you marry him, Ma? We could have done okay without him!*

"Save your breath, Alice. He's not listening to you any more than he ever does. Just sits around all day, daydreaming about God knows what. I suppose he's got some fool idea about being some rock singer or something with a guitar."

Danny couldn't let that remark pass unanswered. "Who told you that?" he demanded angrily, feeling himself redden. His whole body burned. Playing the guitar was something he didn't want anyone to know about, especially Clyde. The guitar was Hank Thompson's. Hank was taking lessons from a man in Belmont.

"Can I try it?" Danny had asked Hank the first time he saw the guitar.

"Sure. I'll teach you what I know, if you want," Hank had assured him. He was two years older than Danny and more like an older brother than a friend. Danny's father and Hank's father had been friends since they were boys; and when Danny's father was alive, the four of them spent a lot of time together, camping out, fishing, or just hanging around.

Before long, Danny was picking out tunes on the guitar. It just happened, as if his fingers had a mind of their own. A couple of times a week he'd go over to Hank's and practice, even if Hank wasn't there. Mrs. Thompson never minded. For the first time in a long time, Danny had something that was important to him. Something he wanted to do. He made up his mind he was going to get a guitar of his own someday. And maybe when he was sixteen he'd quit school and go to Boston or New York and become a guitar player in a rock band. But that was all inside his head. He didn't tell anyone that. Not Willy or Brian or even Hank. Nobody.

"Al Thompson mentioned it to me just yesterday," Clyde answered. "He says Hank's been teaching you. Hank thinks you're real good. Thinks you got a natural talent." Clyde smiled, but he couldn't hide the disapproval in his voice. "Now guitar playing is fine," he went on, "but it ain't life, boy. Most things that come easy are kind of like icing on the cake, if you know what I mean. Not all things we gotta do are so nice and easy, but they gotta be done, like it or not—like this slaughtering. It's a fact of life, boy, and you best get used to it. Now, I told Cliff Strang I'd be ready by six if he got the cow to me. What do you say, Danny?"

Without looking at Clyde, Danny shot back, "I'm not slaughtering. I'm never gonna slaughter. Never! I hate it! I hate that stinking smokehouse."

Clyde reached for him, grabbing Danny by the shoulders. "I say you're helping me, and by God you are! I'm tired of you looking on my work like it's dirty, see. It's a decent job and a decent living. If it's good enough for me, it's good enough for you!"

Danny tried to pull free of Clyde, but Clyde tightened his hold. "Now, you helping me tomorrow or do I gotta beat some sense into you?"

"Clyde, let him go!" Mrs. Grady cried.

"It's about time I done this!" Clyde shouted back. "Look at him! Thirteen and good for nothing but picking at some guitar. If you ask me, he's not gonna grow into a man unless I take him in tow. Now, you better get some sleep, boy. You and me got a date tomorrow morning."

Danny raced out of the kitchen and up the stairs to his room. *I hate him. I hate him! If my fa-*

ther . . . But his father was dead and Clyde was alive. He had to live with Clyde—for the next few years anyway. *But I'm gonna get you back for this, Clyde. Someday I'm gonna get you back.*

Danny stood by the window, gripping the windowsill, breathing in the cool, sweet-smelling air. He gazed out over the moonlit field and his eyes became fixed on the tall grass swaying in the breeze: a monstrous shadow loomed threateningly before him but he laughed fearlessly. When he was small, the moving shadows of the field at night terrified him, haunting him as he lay in bed, in the darkness, trying to fall asleep. Then he'd call for Pterodactyl, and the flying dinosaur would come swooping from his resting place high in the top of the oak to chase away the phantoms. How much simpler it had been then, when all he had to fear were the shadowy creatures of the night.

Chapter Four

Sullenly Danny followed Clyde to the truck
Sunday morning, and they drove in silence to
the smokehouse, Danny sitting as far away
from Clyde as possible. Danny could feel a
mixture of fear and hatred bubbling up inside
him—it was so strong he could almost taste it.
He'd show Clyde he wasn't afraid; but he'd
never forgive or forget.

As soon as they reached the smokehouse,
Danny jumped from the truck and ran toward
the pig sties.

"Where you going?" Clyde called out.

"I was just gonna look at the pigs."

"Don't go wandering. I see a van headed this way. Probably the Strangs'."

"I *ain't* wandering," Danny grumbled and continued over to the sties. He was staring at the baby pigs squealing and kicking to get their mother's milk, when the van pulled up in front of the smokehouse.

"Morning, Cliff," he heard Clyde say, and he felt sick to his stomach. When Clyde called, "Come here, boy," Danny had a desperate urge to run off into the meadow behind the sties and keep running until he reached the highway. Then he'd thumb a ride to Boston.

"Danny!"

"Coming."

Clyde put his arm around Danny and said proudly, "Cliff, this is my boy, Danny. He's gonna help me with your cow."

"Looks kind of young." Mr. Strang smiled.

"He's learning. He's a fast learner, I'll tell you."

It took all of Danny's self-control not to pull away.

"Well, let's get started," Mr. Strang said as he opened up the back of the van. The cow was lying down, and she mooed and groaned in pain as Mr. Strang, Clyde and Danny pulled at her to get her moving.

"Poor, dumb thing," Mr. Strang lamented. "Hate to do this. She was one of my best milkers. The bull got loose in the meadow and near started a stampede. She tripped, I guess."

"It's a shame," Clyde agreed.

Danny was surprised Mr. Strang didn't leave as soon as they got the cow to the slaughterhouse. He couldn't imagine why anyone would stay and watch if he didn't have to. But Mr. Strang was clearly staying. He and Clyde were talking about farm problems as Clyde got ready. Danny watched Clyde choose a knife and sharpen it. Mr. Strang patted the cow's sides reassuringly and talked gently to her.

"You come closer and watch, Danny," Clyde said in a friendly way. "You're gonna be doing this someday."

Mechanically Danny walked toward Clyde and the cow. The moment Clyde lifted the knife, Danny shut his eyes. When he opened them again, it was over. The cow was dead. Danny took a deep breath and swallowed.

"Fast and painless. You're a pro, Clyde," Mr. Strang congratulated him. "You let me know when she's ready now. Like it all wrapped up for freezing."

"Sure thing, Cliff. My wife will give you a call."

"Good seeing you again," Mr. Strang said

and turned to leave. Then he looked at Danny. "You make sure you do a good job on her. She was a good one."

"Yes, sir, Mr. Strang," Danny muttered.

As soon as Mr. Strang left, Clyde said, "Okay, boy, let's get to work." He handed Danny one of the big knives. "I'm gonna open her up. You keep a watchful eye."

Danny's eyes began to blur as Clyde made a slit down the cow's belly.

"Come over here, boy. I want you to make this cut here."

Danny felt as if he were in some kind of a dream as he walked over and knelt beside Clyde and the cow.

"You watching?"

Danny nodded. He could hear Clyde's voice explaining exactly what he wanted Danny to do, but Danny couldn't make his ears listen any more than he could make his eyes watch. Finally he felt Clyde grab his hand with the knife in it. He felt Clyde guide his hand down inside the cow. It was warm and wet . . . and Danny vomited.

~

Beth came down to breakfast wearing her hiking boots, with her canteen slung over her shoulder.

"Well, where are you off to—as if I couldn't guess!" her father greeted her.

Her mother turned from the stove to look at Beth. "Where *are* you going?"

"Hiking," Beth answered, adjusting her hearing aid.

"No, Beth. I don't think so. Your father and I have much too much to do to get this place livable again. I thought you were going to help."

"Oh," Beth sighed, dropping the canteen on the chair. "I forgot. But afterward—then can I go?"

"I don't see why not." Her father nodded.

"Ben, I thought you were going to fix the porch. The whole thing is going to collapse on us. . . ." Mrs. Hampton began.

"That's okay. Daddy doesn't have to go with me. I want to go alone."

"Alone! No, Beth, I don't think so."

"But you promised! Daddy, you said I could go up the mountain alone this year!"

"We said we'd think about it," her mother corrected her.

"I think she's old enough," Mr. Hampton said.

"Well, I don't! She's deaf. Or have you forgotten?"

"For God's sake, Carol, that has nothing to do with going on the mountain."

"It has everything to do with it!" Mrs. Hampton said, pouring herself a cup of coffee.

"Do you think I'd consider letting Beth go on the mountain alone if I thought it was dangerous? She knows the trail as well as anyone. We've been up and down the mountain a hundred times."

"But what if she wanders off?" Mrs. Hampton demanded.

"I won't, Mom. I promise."

Her mother sipped her coffee, looking thoughtful, as if she were considering the question; but finally she said, "I'm sorry, Beth. I'm just not ready to make a decision on this now. I think your father and I have to talk about it more. Another couple of days won't hurt."

"Beth, you and I can go up together, soon," her father promised.

"But I want to go alone. It's not fair. You said I could."

"We never said you could positively. Now, I don't want to talk about it anymore. First things come first, like the house. And the garden. We have to get the garden in. The mountain isn't going to disappear."

"Your mother's right, Beth." Mr. Hampton smiled.

Beth didn't smile back. She didn't feel like it. They had made her a promise. And now they were breaking it. It wasn't fair. She'd been planning on going up the mountain alone today, her first day back.

~

It was only eight o'clock when Danny ran from the smokehouse, but he felt as if he'd been up for days. His hands and shirt were bloodied. Clyde's voice was still echoing in his ears.

"Get out of here!" Clyde bellowed finally. "Your mother could help me better than you!"

Danny didn't care how he looked or smelled. He had to get away from there—away from the cow and away from Clyde and his curses. He knew this was going to happen—he'd known it all along, but at least he had tried. Clyde wouldn't remember that though—the trying. All he'd remember was the failing. And he'd remember it and remember it.

"Puked like a girl all over the cow!" Danny imagined Clyde announcing to everyone. Word would get around, Danny was sure of that.

He stopped at a stream to wash his hands and face. Taking a drink from the muddy water, he swished it around in his mouth, and spit it onto the grass. He soaked his shirt in the stream and laid it out to dry. The bloodstains hadn't washed out, but at least they didn't look so much like blood anymore.

Lying back on the stream bank, he thought about what to do next. The most important thing was to tell Willy and Brian about the cow before they heard it from anyone else. Danny and Willy had been tight for a couple of years now, more or less tolerating Brian and letting him tag along when they felt like it; but lately Danny had sensed Willy easing him out, confiding more and more in Brian, and using Danny for the brunt of his jokes, looking for ways to trip him up and make him look foolish. This thing with the cow was something big Willy could use, so Danny had to stay one step ahead of him.

I'll make a joke of it, Danny decided finally. "Yeah, sure, I puked," he'd say. "But you would have, too, Willy, if you'd been there. It was a gasser—puking all over the cow's guts." Willy would get a charge out of that.

By the time his shirt had dried and he started walking to Willy's, Danny felt almost happy. The day didn't have to be a total loss. It was still early. Maybe Willy would want to do something today, like go up to the old fire tower.

Chapter Five

"You see how quickly the job gets done when we work together?" Mrs. Hampton asked, smiling at Beth. "It's only nine-thirty, and the whole kitchen is set up. You have the rest of the day to do what you want." She crushed and folded the last of the empty cartons and tied it up with the others. "You take these out to the garbage, Beth, and then I think that's the end of it. For the kitchen anyway."

"Can I go then?"

"Where are you off to?"

"Into town."

"What for? Nothing's open but the market and the candy store."

"I can say hello to Mr. and Mrs. Willard and Peggy Dwyer."

"Well, all right—but just don't go making a pest of yourself."

"I won't," Beth sighed.

"And if you see Mary Abelson or that other girl . . . What's her name?"

"Frances."

"That's it. Frances Dumont."

"Mom, I'm not going to see them," Beth said impatiently. All last summer her mother had bugged her about playing with those girls. It annoyed Beth that she was starting the same thing all over now.

"I was only suggesting," her mother said. "Why don't you go by way of the Abelsons'. Maybe you might see Mary."

"Mom! I can pick out my own friends."

"That would be fine, if you did. But you don't. . . ."

Beth turned away so she wouldn't have to read her mother's lips, but Mrs. Hampton stamped her foot angrily. Beth felt the vibrations and reluctantly looked back. "Don't turn away when I'm speaking to you, Beth!"

"I know what you're going to say already! Do

this. Do that. You're always telling me what to do!"

"What's going on in there?" Mr. Hampton called from the porch.

"Ben, why don't you come in here and talk to her. I can't make her understand anything."

"Understand what?" Mr. Hampton asked, putting his arm around Beth.

Beth looked at him.

"Are you still upset about the mountain?" he asked.

Beth frowned. "I just want to go into town and Mom wants me to play with kids I don't like."

Mr. Hampton shook his head. "I still don't understand."

Her mother explained, "I was just telling her that I didn't think it was a good idea for her to go into town on a Sunday and hang around Willards' and the candy store. She's going to turn into a little pest."

"I don't think that's fair, Carol," Mr. Hampton said. "People are always telling me how much they enjoy Beth's company."

"Honestly, Ben, what else are they going to say? But how would you like it if you were trying to run a business, and you had children hanging around the store all morning?"

Beth was carefully reading her parents' lips, and now she cried out bitterly, "Especially if they're deaf."

"Nobody said that, Beth—" her father began.

"Well, Ben, it's true!" Mrs. Hampton sighed. "It's a reality for goodness sakes, and we might as well deal with it. A person has to look at Beth to talk with her. You can't just go about your business and carry on a conversation. It's diverting, and Beth should be aware of it."

"Then why don't you let me go to the mountain?" Beth shouted at her mother. "Then I won't embarrass you!"

"Control yourself, Beth. I can't understand a word when you shout."

"I don't care!" Sometimes her mother made her so angry, she wanted to shake her.

"Are you finished shouting yet?" Mrs. Hampton demanded, taking Beth by the shoulder. "Do you think we can have a civilized discussion?"

With you? Beth felt like asking, but she didn't. Instead she said, "Can I go now?"

"You don't think you're leaving after an outburst like that?" her mother asked.

"You don't understand anything! You're always making me do things. Like play with those girls. I hate them!"

"That's ridiculous. You don't even know them to hate them. You never give other children a chance. I think those girls would be your friends if you weren't so rude. I remember they came over to talk to you quite a few times at the lake last summer."

"That's because *you* talked to them first and invited them over to the blanket. It's true. I know it, and I hate it. I hate it when you do things like that."

"Somebody's got to make the effort," Mrs. Hampton insisted. "Otherwise you'd waste your whole summer wandering around town and hanging around the field."

"You two are never going to work this out," Mr. Hampton said. "Besides, I think Beth has a point, Carol. If she's happy doing whatever it is she does, that's what counts."

"Oh, Ben!" Mrs. Hampton said furiously. "Anything to make Beth happy!"

"Isn't that the point?" he went on, and Beth could tell by the red creeping up his neck that he was getting angry. "We're only here for the summer."

"That child is the way she is because of your attitude!" Mrs. Hampton shot back, her lips twisting and her face getting tight and pinched.

Beth looked away. She hated it when her

parents argued. Their anger changed them into strangers. It was ugly and frightening as she watched them spitting out the angry, awful words. Her father's face grew red and little beads of perspiration formed on his head. Her mother's eyes almost closed, and her hands flew around her head as if she were shooing away a bee. It was always terrible when they fought, but worse when they fought over her.

Beth sat at the kitchen table, but she didn't look at her parents now. She didn't want to know what they were saying. Instead, she stared at the tile on the kitchen floor, following the geometric pattern as if it were a maze, until she felt her father touching her.

"Have you done everything your mother wanted?" he asked, trying to smile, but Beth knew he was still upset.

She looked at her mother. "Have I?"

Her mother nodded abruptly.

"Then you can go into town, if that's what you want," her father went on.

Beth looked anxiously at her mother.

"Go on. But just remember what I said."

"I will," Beth murmured, and hurried outside to get her bike, then remembered there was no air in the tires. This wasn't a good time to ask for the bicycle pump, so she started walking into town.

She hadn't gone far, when a car stopped. The driver leaned out the window and waved. It was Mr. McCowan.

"When did you get back?" he asked.

"Last night," Beth answered, running to the car.

"Want a ride someplace?"

"No. I'm going into town. I think I want to walk."

"Okay," Mr. McCowan smiled. "You tell your dad for me that I'm going to get him to come fishing this summer for sure."

"I will," she promised and waved to Mr. McCowan as he drove off.

She was glad she hadn't accepted Mr. McCowan's offer of a ride. The walk into town made her feel better.

She stopped to pick some wildflowers growing along the road. *She will let me go up the mountain. She won't. She will let me go up the mountain. She won't. . . .* she said to herself as she pulled off their petals one at a time. The first flower ended on *She won't,* so Beth played the game with another. The second time it ended with *She will.* And so did the third. When the fourth ended with *She won't,* she put the few remaining flowers behind her ear.

Main Street was deserted when Beth arrived, reminding her of a picture on a postcard, and for that moment it belonged to only her. As she neared the Willards' market, she noticed rows of vegetable and flower plants in front of the store, the kind her mother bought for the garden every year.

I'll have to remember to tell Mom about the plants, she thought. *That'll make her happy.*

She waved to Clem Cintron and Mr. Willard, who were talking in front of the market, and then to the Misses Dawson as they drove by in their old black car her father said was an antique now. When she got to the candy store, she tried to peek in, but the window was as dirty as ever, and Beth couldn't see a thing.

"Well, Beth!" Peggy Dwyer exclaimed when Beth walked in. "I thought I might see you soon. How was your winter?"

"Okay. But it's better here," Beth told her, reaching into her pocket for a quarter. "Have any peppermint stick?"

"Now you put away your money," Peggy insisted. "The first ice cream of the summer is my treat."

Peggy sat with Beth at the counter and told her all the town news: Mrs. Winston had a boy in May. Harvey Garth broke his ankle and had to have it set three times. Susan Whimple married Harry Swan and wasn't that a surprise to everyone? And John Goodwin bought a new

Cadillac, and nobody knew where he got the money for it.

After a while Beth grew tired of Peggy's talk. Her thoughts turned to the mountain. It was almost a relief to get outside again; but she didn't feel like going home so soon. Maybe her parents would still be angry with each other. Besides, there was nothing to do at home. . . . Her mother was being so dumb. Nothing could happen to her on the mountain. *Well, maybe she'll change her mind soon,* Beth hoped as she crossed Main Street and hurried past the monument of the Revolutionary War hero. *If only I could go hiking today. It's so hot. The trail is probably the only cool, shady place, besides the lake.* But she couldn't go to the lake either because she couldn't go swimming alone.

As she cut up through the woods to the main road, Mt. Ash came into sight again, looming like a peaceful giant over the valley, and Beth was filled with a feeling of coming home, as exciting as meeting an old friend again, someone she'd longed to see all winter. If only her mother could understand how important these feelings were, then she would understand why Beth could never be lonely here, why she didn't need friends here, at least not friends as she had in the city.

A feeling of nervous excitement made her

run—as she had run through the field yesterday. The mountain was always with her: she
could see it from her window, the field, the
swing, town and the road. Beth knew she
should go home, but she couldn't. She'd waited
all winter to climb the mountain. She couldn't
wait any longer.

Chapter Six

The trail marker read: "Mt. Ash. Fordhook trail. 1.3 miles." A sudden rush of anticipation made Beth shiver. The Fordhook trail was her favorite. Maybe she'd climb all the way to the top. Maybe she'd even climb to the old tower. If she hurried, it wouldn't take too long. The trail was shaded almost to the top and a stream crossed it partway up. It began as a flat path but gradually grew steeper until, about half-way, it became very steep, rocky, and rutted with the roots of trees. The climbing was harder there, but Beth liked it that way. Just after the really steep part, another trail cut off to the right, leading to some caves. Beth's father told her that Indians might have used the caves for hideouts, and when Beth was younger, she and her father had pretended all kinds of adventures there.

Beth wanted to go to the caves now, but it would take an extra twenty minutes, and she had to save time to climb the fire tower. On a day like today, you could see forever from the tower.

She knew the trail by heart, where it suddenly grew steep, where to find the fallen tree looking like an alligator, and where the trees ended. When she reached the open sunny part, she knew she was almost to the top. There was only the big patch of blueberry bushes and then the turn-off leading to the old tower. Once Beth reached the turn-off, she began running.

Sometimes her father didn't climb all the eighty-nine steps of the tower, but Beth always did—the old, creaky ladder made the climb more scary, and Beth loved it. Even on a hot day there was wind, once you climbed to about the fifty-third step. But it was windiest inside the lookout at the top. Some of the windows had been broken, and the wind whipped through it so fiercely sometimes Beth thought the tower would blow down; her father promised it would take more than just a summer breeze to topple it.

The first thing Beth did when she got to the lookout was check that her name was still on the wall with all the others. It was. Then she folded her arms across one of the windowsills and stared out. From the tower the mountains seemed to go on and on like the sea until, at the end, they melted into the sky. Everything was different up here. The air, so still everywhere else, blew through the broken windows like the wind of a storm. The gigantic mountains seemed so close she could almost reach out and touch the next peak—only a hop, skip and a jump, *for a giant anyway,* she giggled.

Here Beth was on top of the world, a beautiful exciting world belonging for the moment only to her and the mountain. It made her feel so special even the possibility of her mother's anger couldn't spoil it. She was glad she'd come up the mountain alone. If only she didn't have to lie about being here—then she could stay on top of her world as long as she wanted, and when she got home, she could share it all with her father.

~

Willy made a retching sound as he heaved a handful of muddy leaves in Danny's direction. Seeing it coming, Danny jumped back, but not in time. The wet mass landed on his neck and shoulder. Brian and Willy laughed hysterically.

"Funny. Real funny!" Danny shot back, yanking off the muddy leaves and throwing them on the ground.

"A little cow guts never hurt no one," Willy teased.

"You should be used to it by now," Brian added.

"Knock it off!" Danny shouted, feeling himself ready to explode. All the way up the mountain Willy and Brian had been at him about the cow. Sure, they'd laughed when Danny first told them. The problem was they hadn't stopped laughing.

"Right, anything you say," Willy answered sarcastically, edging closer to Danny until his face was inches away. Then Willy opened his mouth and pretended to vomit. "Sorry. The sight of guts always makes me puke."

"Leave it alone, Willy!" Danny screamed, shoving Willy with all his strength. If Brian hadn't been standing behind him, Willy would have fallen.

Willy was startled. His grin vanished. "Hey,

Danny, what's the big deal? I mean, I didn't know you took this thing so serious."

What's the matter with me? Danny asked himself as he and Willy stood cautiously eyeing each other. *Here Willy's joking about the cow just like I wanted him to do and I gotta go and make a big deal out of it!* He knew he had to do something fast before Willy got mad and the situation got out of hand.

Breaking into a grin, Danny quickly said, "Hey, Willy, I'm sorry. You're right. The whole thing is real funny. It's Clyde. I guess he got to me more than I thought." As he spoke, Danny bent over and scooped up a handful of mud and leaves. "Here, have some guts!" he laughed as he threw them at Willy, then raced up the trail before Willy could retaliate.

Willy and Brian chased after him but they didn't catch up until they reached the fire tower. Willy stopped short. "Hey, Danny, ain't that the dummy coming down the ladder? You know, the kid who lives across the field from you?"

Danny looked up. Beth was in the middle of the ladder, slowly and cautiously making her way down.

"Yeah, it is," Danny said.

"Come on. We can have a little fun!" Willy

laughed as he ran to the ladder, shaking it furiously.

"What are you doing?" Danny cried, and he pulled Willy's hands off the ladder. "Are you crazy? She could fall and break her neck!"

"What's with you, Danny boy? I was just giving the dummy a scare or two. If you don't want to, Brian does. Don't you, Brian?"

"Sure thing, Willy!" And Willy and Brian began shaking the ladder again.

"Come on, Willy . . ." Danny began.

Willy turned angrily on him, looking hateful and disgusted. "Hey, lay off, you creep!" he screamed, shaking the ladder harder than ever.

Shocked by Willy's open hostility, Danny stepped back as if obeying a command. He watched Beth on the ladder as she fiercely grasped the sides, frantically looking first up to the tower and then down to the ground. He knew he should do something to help her; but he knew he couldn't. So he did nothing.

Beth's heart was beating so fast she could feel it in her throat. She tried moving her foot down to the next rung but it seemed impossible. She was frozen where she stood. Up or down? Up looked so far away, but down— those boys were down there, waiting for her. It was hard to make them out. Why were they doing this? What would they do when she got down? If she got down. How would she get down? *The shaking. The terrible shaking. If only they would stop!* If only she could get her body to move. If only the shaking would stop. It was so far down.

"Daddy! Daddy!" she found herself screaming and screaming, and still the ladder kept shaking.

Then the shaking stopped—only for a few moments, but enough for Beth to take the first steps. *Keep going, keep going. You can make it. Keep going,* she ordered herself.

It seemed like a mile between each rung, but slowly, so slowly, Beth made her way down to the bottom. When she was only a few feet away, a hand reached up and grabbed her. It was Danny, trying to help, but his touch so frightened Beth she pulled away, tumbling to the ground.

She screamed, more from hatred than fear or pain, and sprang up, ready to attack her attackers. She was going to get them back. Brian was closest, and she leaped at him, but Willy caught her from behind, holding her arms tightly. She kicked wildly, trying to break free.

"Let her go!" Danny shouted.

"Okay, sure, Danny boy. I'll let the dummy go, just for you!" Willy taunted.

As he dropped his hands, Beth leaped at Danny. He jumped out of her reach.

"Gee, Danny. The dummy don't appreciate all you're trying to do for her." Willy laughed.

"That's 'cause she's just a dummy! I wonder why she's got that hearing aid anyway! It sure don't seem to do her any good!" Brian laughed.

It was impossible for Beth to read the boys' lips now, but their laughing faces drove her mad. First they had terrified her and now they were making fun of her, waving their arms, making faces, laughing. . . . She went madly after each of them in turn, but always they jumped back in time.

"Come on, let's get out of here," Willy finally announced. "This is boring." He and Brian started to run back down to the Fordhook trail.

Too exhausted to move, Beth stood with her arms hanging by her sides, gasping for breath.

Danny stayed behind, staring at her, listening to the terrible sounds of her crying, and he wanted to help her. She looked so scared. Little and scared and deaf . . .

"Coming?" Willy's voice demanded from down the trail.

"Come on," Brian echoed. "We gotta get out of here."

"Yeah, I'm coming," he called and looked at

Beth once more. "I'm sorry," he said even though he knew she couldn't understand him.

Beth didn't notice Danny had stayed behind. She was staring at the ground, numb, tired, wondering what to do next. It was late. She'd been gone so long—her mother would be worrying by now. She had to get home fast but home seemed so far away. *Why did I ever come?* she cried, and tears began streaming down her face. She stood on the mountain top until she had no more tears to cry. Then she started home.

She'd seen the boys go off toward the Fordhook, so Beth chose another trail down, longer than the Fordhook, but safer; and she ran all the way. By the time she reached the bottom of the mountain, her throat was parched, and her skin burned as if she'd been attacked by thousands of tiny arrows. The heat of the mid-day sun seemed to be exploding inside her head, and her feet felt numb and heavy in the sweltering boots; but she had to keep running—she had to get home.

Taking the short cut through the field, she saw her parents working in the garden before they saw her.

"Hello!" she called when she reached the edge of the field.

Mrs. Hampton waved. "You were gone so

long!" she said when Beth reached the garden. "Did you spend some time with Mary and Frances?"

Mary and Frances! They were the people furthest from her mind. *Why are you asking about them?* Sighing deeply to catch her breath, she shook her head hesitantly. "I was just talking to people. First I met Mr. McCowan. He said he wants to go fishing with you, Daddy. And then I was talking to Peggy. She talks forever. But I wasn't bothering her. Nobody else was in the store." Beth spoke quickly, nervously, and her words slurred together.

"Are you all right, Beth?" her mother asked.

Beth began shaking inside. Did her mother sense her lie? If it hadn't been for those horrible boys, none of this would be happening, her day wouldn't be ruined. If only her head would stop hurting, so she could think. "Yes, I'm fine. I just have a headache. . . ." And she couldn't go on. She was going to cry.

"What's wrong, Beth?" her father asked, hurrying to her.

Barely able to understand him through the tears, she took a deep breath and sighed, "I'm okay."

"You don't look well. Your face is flushed. You're all upset. Something happened," her mother insisted.

Beth shook her head violently. "No. I . . . I was running, that's all. And now I have a terrible headache."

"Well, no wonder. You don't run in heat like this!" her mother exclaimed.

"I was gone so long. I thought you would worry."

"I'm glad to know you were thinking about us, but you shouldn't have run in this heat. Why don't you go into the house and lie down? There's some lemonade," Mrs. Hampton began and then put down her shovel. "Come on. You look like you're having a heat stroke. I'll help you wash up."

Beth didn't argue. She wanted her mother now. She needed her soft cool hands to wipe away the sweaty, matted hair from her forehead. She needed her mother to care for her. As Mrs. Hampton rubbed the ice cold glass of lemonade against Beth's cheeks and throbbing head, it was all Beth could do not to reach out and grab her, hold her tightly, and tell her what the boys had done. The memory of the terrifying climb down the ladder and the shock of being pulled to the ground seemed as real to her now as when it had happened. She could almost feel again the humiliation and anger as the boys had laughed at her, their mouths opening and closing in ugly mockery. Now as she remembered it all, she began shaking inside. She needed someone soft and close to hold her tightly. She needed to bury her head against her mother until the shaking stopped.

Maybe her mother had been right after all—being deaf did make a difference. If she could hear, if she wasn't different, the boys wouldn't have picked on her and tormented her. *I hate being deaf!* she wanted to cry to her mother; but instead she leaned against her and said, "My head hurts. It hurts so bad."

And her mother stroked her gently, kissing her softly on the head.

Chapter Seven

"See you," Danny mumbled as he got on his bike and started down the road.

"Yeah, sure," was all Willy said.

Those were the first words Willy and Danny had spoken all the way down the mountain. It was weird. The whole hike down had been weird: Willy and Brian laughing and joking and Danny silently following a few steps behind. There had been no wisecracks about the dummy or the cow. There had been no communication. It was as if Danny didn't exist.

The silence, the nothingness—it seemed to

speak more loudly to Danny than any words could. It was over between him and Willy. Danny had felt it coming. It had been building up for a while; but he hadn't thought it would end like this. Something had happened on the mountain. Maybe it was the muddy leaves. Maybe it was Beth. Maybe it was both of them, and maybe it was none of them. It didn't matter. Something had come between them suddenly, swiftly, and yet absolutely. Both boys understood it, but it was too unexpected to deal with now. Another time they would have it out.

Mrs. Grady was sitting on the porch when Danny rode into the driveway. Their eyes met and the memory of Clyde and the cow flashed before him. Danny looked away, ashamed.

"You all right?" his mother asked apprehensively; and he knew she knew everything.

"Clyde told you about the cow, huh?"

Holding out her hands toward him, she asked, "Where have you been, Danny? I've been worried sick about you. Clyde said you left the smokehouse in an awful state. Why didn't you come home?"

Home—it was strange but he never once thought of coming home. He should have. He wished he had.

"Come and sit down next to me, Danny. We can talk."

Her voice sounded so soft and understanding, comforting, and Danny wanted to rush to her. But he couldn't do that. He had to be strong. So he leaned against the porch railing and said as carelessly as he could, "Is Clyde still mad?"

"We talked. He's calmed down some."

Danny sensed a sadness in her voice, and he noticed how tired and worried she looked. "I'm sorry I didn't come home, Ma. I was just messing around with Willy and Brian. I should have come home," he apologized.

Clasping her hands together, Mrs. Grady shook her head and sighed. "It's a shame it happened. It's just a shame. . . ."

"I couldn't help it, Ma! I told you I couldn't do it!" he burst out.

"I know, Danny. I'm not blaming you."

Danny waited for her to say more, to defend him and blame Clyde, but she didn't. She sat fussing with a loose button on her blouse. *She sides with Clyde!* he screamed inside his head, and waited again for her to say something to ease his anguish. Her silence maddened him. He felt like grabbing her and demanding, finally, *What are we doing with him, Ma? We're not Grady. We're Haines! You don't love him—not the way you loved Dad.* And he remembered what she'd told him just before she'd married Clyde.

"Nobody will take the place of your father—or you, Danny. You'll always come first with me."

"Then why do I have to have his name, Ma?" he'd pleaded. "I'm Haines. It's Dad's name. I want it."

She'd put her arms around him and cried silent tears, whispering, "You'll always be your father's son, Danny. Nobody can take that from you, and nobody wants to. But Clyde wants you to have his name. It's important to him. He wants us all to be a family—not just him and me, but the three of us."

I don't want his name! I don't want him! Danny had wanted to tell her, but he couldn't. His mother had suffered so much when his father died. He remembered her tears, her pain, the way she held him that terrible night as they sat in the darkness, the way she squeezed him as she cried. Sometimes the cries were only moans as she wrapped her arms around him so tightly he hurt; but he never moved or left her that night. And when he cried, he cried more for her than for his father or himself. His father was dead. It didn't seem real, not nearly so real as his mother's pain.

That night he promised himself he'd never do anything to make her cry again. That's why he'd taken Clyde's name. That's why he never

told her how much he hated Clyde. But sometimes that promise seemed so hard to keep, like
now, when he thought she'd forgotten all she'd
said about her love, when she let Clyde come
first.

She reached out for his hand, and Danny felt
warmed by her touch, suddenly certain she was
going to say all the things he wanted to hear.
But she didn't; instead she told him, "Clyde
tries so hard with you, Danny. I know you
don't see it, but he only wants what's best for
you."

Danny's body went rigid. His hand grew suddenly cold in hers and he trembled.

"Danny, what's wrong?" she began, but she
said no more for the screen door opened, and
Clyde came out.

"So, Danny, you're home. Your Ma's been
worried about you. You shouldn't have run off
like that."

All the hurt, anger and confusion of the
day—of the cow, Willy, Beth, his mother—
rushed over him at the sound of Clyde's voice.
He couldn't speak even if he wanted.

Squeezing Danny's hand reassuringly, Mrs.
Grady said, "I wasn't all that worried now."

"Still, the boy should have come back sooner,
Alice."

"I know. But he's here now. No sense making a fuss," she warned Clyde.

Clyde coughed and said, "Well, maybe you're right." Walking toward Danny he added, "So, you all right, boy? I guess things got a little out of hand this morning." As he spoke, he put his hand on Danny's shoulder.

Danny pulled away in disgust. "Leave me alone!"

"Now, Danny . . ." he heard his mother say.

"No! No! I don't want to hear any more!" Danny cried. "I don't want you telling me how good he is to me or how much he wants us to be a family. All he knows is pigs and slitting their throats."

"Danny, Danny . . ." his mother was pleading with him, trying to put her arms around him, but Danny pushed her away.

"Now, take it easy, boy," Clyde said nervously. "I know you're upset, but crying and screaming's no way to act. Come on, it's time you and me talked. You know, man to man like."

Danny laughed, a loud, high-pitched, crazed laugh. "You and me talk? Are you crazy, Clyde? There's nothing in this whole world I gotta talk to you about!"

"Danny, you have to calm down and talk

sense," his mother insisted. She wasn't soft and understanding anymore. She didn't feel his pain.

"I'm your son, Ma. Don't you care about me?"

"You're talking nonsense, Danny. Just pure nonsense. Of course I care about you. That's not the question here at all. Clyde was upset about what happened this morning. We've been talking and talking about it."

"I don't care what he's got to say!"

"Well, it's time you started caring, Danny!" she told him angrily.

"No, Ma! Never!"

"Stop it!" Clyde shouted suddenly. "Now, I've had it from you, boy. I've had about all I can take. I know it was hard on you when I married your mother. I understood you didn't like the idea of my coming and taking over your father's place, but I figured in time you'd change your mind. But you've been so dead set against me from the very start, you've never been willing to give me a chance."

"Clyde, don't. Don't say things you'll regret."

"How can I regret anything I say to that boy when the only thing that'd make him happy is to see me gone?"

"That's not true, Clyde." she insisted.

"Of course, it's true, Alice. We all know it. There's nothing in this whole world I can do to make that boy feel any different about me. And I'll tell you something else. I'm not sorry for what happened this morning. Maybe it's more of that kind of experience that Danny needs. I just realized it ain't enough giving him my name. I've been so worried these past years about him not liking me that I just let him run wild. I ain't given him any guidance. But things are gonna change around here, boy. So long as I'm the provider in this house, you'll do as I say. You can hate me all you want so long as you do as I say. Is that clear?"

"Clyde, this isn't the time—" Mrs. Grady began.

"Then when *is* the time? You gonna go on coddling that boy for the rest of his life because his father died?"

"Clyde!"

"No, now you listen to me, Alice. I've been thinking about this for a while now, but I've never said anything because it didn't seem like my place. But I see now it is my place because there's not another living person who's gonna say it. It's time you and Danny both accepted the fact that Andy died and let's get on with life from there. Do you think your father would like to see you now, boy? Well, I don't think so. Just what would you tell him if he asked you, 'So what you been doing with your life lately, son?' What could you say. 'Oh, nothing much. I mess around with my friends some. Pick a little at a guitar, but other than that I don't do much. I don't even help Ma clean up the dishes after dinner.' Now what do you think your father would say to that?"

"My father wouldn't have made me slaughter any cow!" Danny shouted. "My father wouldn't have slaughtered any cow either. My father—"

"Well, maybe that's the case, boy. Maybe it is. But the fact is, I'm your father now. And I'm a pig farmer, and that means slaughtering hogs, like it or not. And you're my son, Danny Grady, and that means you gotta help me out. You understand me, boy?"

"I'm no son of yours!"

"Danny, don't," his mother cried.

"No, Alice. He's right. When I married you, I promised I'd bring him up like he was my own. And that's what I aim to do, starting right now. You're my boy, Danny, and I'm your father, and we're gonna start acting like father and son. You understand?"

Danny's head was spinning. He was on the

verge of tears and filled with such a terrible rage he wasn't sure he could control it if Clyde pushed him any further.

"Stop it, Clyde!" Mrs. Grady pleaded. "Let the boy be. Look at him. He's white with fear."

"Well, maybe fear's where we got to start then! Maybe a little fear is just what Danny needs to get him moving and stop him feeling so sorry for himself. All your loving and understanding don't do the boy any good, Alice. He's turning into a mama's boy. That ain't what you want, and it ain't what Andy would have wanted. From now on he'll get up with me in the morning and help feed the hogs and clean out the sties. After you get those chores done, boy, you can sweep out the store so your mother don't have to. And then I'll see what other odds and ends need doing. Slowly you're gonna learn all there is to know about pig farming and the smokehouse, and then you can make a decision about how you feel about it. But so long as you live in this house, you'll do your share of work around here. Now, you see anything wrong with that, Alice?"

Danny held his breath, waiting for his mother's answer. When she said, "No, I agree with you, Clyde," Danny felt numb. There was no longer any anger or pain, only a cold emptiness. He stared blankly at his mother as she went on.

"There's nothing wrong with Danny helping you at the smokehouse. But I want Danny to understand he's not being punished for what happened this morning. You need his help plain and simple."

Clyde thought for a moment. "Well, I guess that's the truth, boy. I want you to know that."

Danny shrugged and started for the kitchen door. "What does it matter?" he mumbled.

Chapter Eight

"Are you making pancakes for breakfast, Mom?" Beth asked as she came into the kitchen.

"Strawberry."

"Wow, what's the special occasion?"

Beth watched her mother glance at her father.

"You tell her, Ben." Mrs. Hampton smiled.

"No, why don't you tell her?" He looked at Beth and winked.

"Tell me what?"

Mrs. Hampton had gone back to the stove so Mr. Hampton began, "Well, your mother thought you would need a big, hearty breakfast today."

"Why? Where are we going?"

"Not 'we' Beth—you. Your mother and I were talking, and we decided you can go up the mountain alone today, if you like. We'll give you a trial, and if it works, and you like it, then you can go whenever you want."

"You mean it!"

Mr. Hampton nodded. "I've pumped up your bike tires. So you're on your own."

"Thank you!" She ran to her father and hugged him and then to her mother.

"But you have to have a time limit," her mother added. "Your father thinks two hours is enough."

"That's plenty! Oh, thank you!" She threw her arms around her mother.

Mrs. Hampton hugged her back, and when Beth looked up, Mrs. Hampton asked, "How many pancakes can you eat?"

Beth suddenly remembered yesterday at the fire tower. Her stomach fluttered nervously, and her excitement began to fade—maybe she shouldn't go on the mountain alone after all. She shook her head.

"How many pancakes can you eat?" her mother repeated.

"Oh, I don't know. Three."

"Three! I've made enough for you to have at least six."

"Oh, okay. Six."

"Something wrong?" her father asked as Beth sat down at the table.

"No . . ."

"You don't have to go on the mountain alone, if that's worrying you."

"It's not," she insisted.

"And you don't have to go today either. You can go anytime you want."

"I know," she said, pouring on the maple syrup. "But I want to go today. I do!"

"Okay, okay!" He laughed. "Then there's no problem."

"No. No problem." Beth mumbled to herself.

Beth rode her bike slowly to the Fordhook trail, arguing with herself as she went: *Do I want to go up the mountain alone? Do I really want to? . . . No, I don't,* and she stopped the bike and thought for a few minutes. *Yes I do,* she finally decided, and got back on her bike and began pedaling. *What's there to be afraid of anyway? I've been hiking with Daddy hundreds of times, and we hardly ever see anyone. Besides, I'm not going to the tower today. I'll go to the caves. Maybe the tower wasn't such a good place to go anyway—*

even if I wasn't deaf. The old ladder is too creaky.
That was a dumb thing to do. . . .

Beth was so lost in thought she didn't even
notice the Clarkes' pickup truck pull over to
the side of the road until she almost crashed
into it. When she looked up, she saw Mrs.
Clarke waving to her. "I thought it was you,
Beth. Welcome back. Jamie was just asking
about you last week."

Beth jumped off her bike and hurried over
to the cab of the truck. "Hi, Mrs. Clarke. Hi,
Jamie!"

Jamie stared at Beth as if she were a
stranger. At first Beth was surprised. She had
spent a lot of time at the Clarkes' farm last
summer, and she and Jamie had been good
friends even though he was three years
younger.

"How are you, Jamie?" Beth tried again.

Jamie still stared.

Mrs. Clarke nudged him. "You're being ter-
ribly impolite, Jamie. Beth asked you how you
are. You must remember Beth."

"That's okay," Beth said. "He probably
doesn't remember how funny I talk."

"You don't talk funny at all, Beth," Mrs.
Clarke insisted. "Does she, Jamie?"

With a blank expression on his face, Jamie
shook his head.

"Well, I think you're talking much better than you did when you left last summer. Isn't she, Jamie?"

Jamie looked from Beth to his mother and nodded silently.

"Honestly, Jamie, I don't know what's gotten into you. Just last week you were asking me when Beth was coming back." She turned to Beth and said apologetically, "I really don't understand that boy sometimes."

"That's okay." Beth smiled and said to Jamie, "I bet you have a lot of new calves. I bet there are at least—"

"Thirteen!" he announced proudly.

"Wow, that's more than last year! Can I come and see them?"

Jamie looked at his mother, and Mrs. Clarke leaned forward again so Beth could see her. "We're very busy this week. How about one day next week?"

"Okay!" Beth nodded.

Mrs. Clarke smiled. "Good. I'll give your mother a call."

As Beth stepped away from the truck, Jamie leaned out the window. "Bye!" he shouted, and he and Beth waved to each other until the truck disappeared around a curve.

As she rode toward the Fordhook trail Beth

thought about the Clarkes' farm: the cows and the big barn with the haylofts, the chickens and the mean old rooster that Mr. Clarke finally had to kill for a Sunday dinner, and the apple orchard with the pond where she and Jamie caught frogs and newts. There were so many things she liked about the farm, but the best was Mrs. Clarke's dollhouse. It was very old and beautiful, with three floors, nine rooms, and a porch filled with all kinds of miniature furniture: tiny rocking chairs and a potbellied stove, a grandfather's clock and a piano with keys that moved up and down. Mrs. Clarke had made a lot of the furniture herself, and even though everything was very fragile, she let Beth play with it. Last summer she'd taught Beth how to make dollhouse people out of clothespins and pipe cleaners.

Beth left her bike at the base of the trail and quickly started up the mountain. After hiking a short while, she lost any fear she had of being on the mountain alone. She was too happy to be afraid. *Those dumb boys—it was just a coincidence,* she assured herself as she waded in a big puddle, wiggling her toes as the mud oozed up between them. When she reached the place where the stream crossed the trail, she splashed in to rinse off, then climbed up and down the big rock formations twice. It was much more fun climbing today than yesterday, because now she didn't have to worry about the time. She could go as fast or as slow as she wanted.

When she reached the turn-off to the caves, Beth didn't hesitate in taking it. She loved exploring the caves, then climbing to the top of the biggest one where she had a wonderful view of the valley. But when she reached the clearing just before the caves, she stopped short. At the edge of the cliff, near the biggest cave, was a mother black bear and her cub rummaging through the bushes for berries. Beth carefully backed up, paused for a moment to watch the bears, and then turned and ran happily back to the trail. She knew of another cliff higher up the mountain which had a view of the caves. She could watch the bears safely from there.

As she hurried up the trail, she thought of the time two years earlier when she and her father had seen another bear. Her mother had been upset when they told her. "I don't think you should go hiking if there are bears!" she insisted.

Beth and her father looked at each other, smiling knowingly. "Bears aren't dangerous," Beth said. "They're more scared of people than we are of them. Right, Daddy?"

"So long as they're left alone. But I'd say we were lucky to see this one. They usually stay pretty well hidden around here."

"Well, just be careful," Mrs. Hampton sighed. And for weeks after, she worried about bears. Once she even suggested Mr. Hampton take a gun with him on a hike.

"What for?" Beth asked.

"Besides, we don't even own one," Mr. Hampton reminded his wife.

"Well, maybe you should get one if you and Beth hike where there are bears."

"Never!" Beth insisted. "We would never shoot a bear, or any animal. We hate hunters!"

And her father had agreed.

After a while, Mrs. Hampton had stopped worrying because Beth and her father didn't see the bear again.

But I better not tell them about this bear, Beth decided. *Mom will get all upset and she won't let me go hiking alone. And I'm not going to do anything to ruin that.*

To Beth's disappointment, the bears were gone when she reached the cliff. With a sigh, she looked out over the valley. In one direction she saw the field, her house, the old oak, and when she squinted her eyes, she imagined she could see the swing. In the other direction she could see all of Main Street.

Everything looked small and unreal from so high up, reminding her of a toy town, as little and perfect as Mrs. Clarke's dollhouse. The people were like specks of dirt, and the cars like beetles. *Wouldn't it be something to have. a whole miniature town just like Main Street?* she thought as she turned once more to look at her house and the swing. She could see the Grady house, too; and a thought crossed her mind, making her giggle. *If only it was a toy town for just a minute, and the people were toy people, too. Then I'd take Danny and Willy and Brian and scrunch them up and throw them in the garbage— wouldn't that be a super way to get them back!*

~

"I'll be in the smokehouse, boy. You come and let me know when you're finished with those chores," Clyde said after he explained the feeding to Danny.

"Yeah, okay," Danny mumbled.

"And be careful of Seymour. He's a mean one," Clyde added, starting toward the smoke-house.

First Danny hosed down the sties, taking delight in squirting the water full force at Seymour. Seymour, who hardly moved except to eat, grunted and glared at Danny through his slitlike eyes, almost hidden under layers of fat. He was so mean and ugly looking—*just the kind of animal Clyde would take a liking to,* Danny thought with a chuckle. His mother was always worrying that Seymour would break loose and hurt somebody, but Clyde refused to turn him into ham. "He's my first and only prizewinner," Clyde would say almost tenderly. "Can't bring myself to slaughter him just yet."

"But don't lie there just resting easy," Danny warned Seymour. "You'll get yours some day. So why don't you give it to Clyde before he gives it to you—you fat, dumb hog!" He laughed, giving Seymour one final squirt.

After Danny finished washing down the other sties and feeding the hogs, he went to find Clyde. "I did everything you told me," he said. "What do you want me to do next?"

Clyde put down the meat he was working on and said, "Well, you could help me cure this ham here, but I don't think you're ready to work with me yet—and I don't expect I'm ready to work with you neither, so, seeing it's Monday and the store's closed, I guess you can do what you want now. But tomorrow morning you check with your ma after you finish with the hogs."

Danny nodded.

"What you got planned for the day?" Clyde asked as Danny started out the door.

"Things."

"Real important things, I guess."

"Not really. Just things."

Clyde started working on the meat as he spoke, "You know, Danny, I was thinking, there never seems to be time to fix all the things that need fixing around here. It gets me down though, and your ma, too. You know how she's always complaining that, just because we keep pigs, it don't mean the place has to look like a pig sty."

"Yeah, I heard her say that."

"Well, I guess she's got a point there. I always put her off, but it gnaws at me a bit. A man's gotta take pride in his business and that means keeping it up. I think your ma would be real pleased if she thought you were pulling this place together."

"Look, Clyde, you got more work for me to do, why don't you just come out and tell me? I mean, I gotta do it. You said it. Ma said it."

"Now, hold on boy. Let's see if we can talk to each other without getting angry and saying ugly things."

"Then just say what you want to say, Clyde."

"Yep, you're right, boy. No sense beating around the bush. See, I was thinking, there's a whole bunch of things that need repairing around here. I'm sure your ma has a list a mile long, but just off the top of my head, I'd say the barn door needs fixing, the sties need repairing, the roof on Seymour's hut will probably cave in come the first snowstorm next winter. The store could use a coat of paint and the barn could do with a cleaning. You know, that's a real nice barn we got there if someone could just pull it together.

"You expect me to do all that?" Danny gasped.

"Nope. I was just thinking that maybe you might like to take on one of those jobs—not like a chore, mind you, more like a project. And if you do a good job, well, I might see my way clear to paying you something. 'Course it can't be much, but it's better than nothing. See, the way I figure, the summer's a long time to just hang around with those friends of yours. Hanging around gets boring, and being bored leads to trouble. But if you were working on a project . . ."

What friends? Danny laughed bitterly to himself, but to Clyde he only shrugged and said, "I don't know. I don't think so—I mean, if I got a choice."

"Yeah, you got a choice. Chores is one thing. There's no choosing when it comes to chores. But don't say no so quickly. I seem to remember your ma saying you're real good with your hands, kind of like Andy."

Danny didn't want to hear Clyde talking about his father now, and he quickly said, "My father could make anything, anything at all. And fix anything, too. There wasn't anything he didn't know how to fix."

Clyde put down his knife. "I know that, Danny, I do. Your ma's showed me all his fine work around the house. I couldn't have done all he did, building those kitchen cabinets and modernizing the kitchen like he did. I guess you're real proud of him."

"I don't need you telling me *nothing* about my father!"

"No, you don't. But if you got a natural talent like that from your father, well, I just thought you might want to put some of it to work. Understand now, you'd be doing this strictly on your own. I wouldn't interfere at all. And besides, it might be fun."

"I don't know, Clyde. I'll think about it," Danny said as he turned to leave again.

"That's fine, boy. Fine. You just think about it."

Danny left without another word, got on his bike and started down the road; but he thought about what Clyde had said. Maybe this idea of a project wasn't so bad. He had nothing else to do. Hank was working in his uncle's hardware store in the Greenway shopping mall. And Danny didn't want anything to do with Willy and Brian—not for a while, anyway.

Besides, it'd be easy fixing up the sties, he assured himself as his bike coasted along the flat road. *And it won't take long. I can knock them off in a week for sure. And do a good job, too—probably better than Clyde. It wouldn't be so bad making a little extra money either. Put it toward the guitar. I wonder what he'll pay me? . . . Maybe I could do the barn, too, if I worked all week. . . .*

Danny thought about going back and telling Clyde he could start today on the sties, but he changed his mind. He didn't want Clyde to think he'd decided so quickly. Besides, if he was going to be working all week, he needed today to himself. *Maybe I'll practice on the guitar,* he thought. *Yeah, I'll go ask Hank now. . . .* And he turned his bike around and headed toward the mall.

~ II ~
The Bears

Chapter Nine

"Why, that's a beautiful job, Danny. Really professional. Don't you think so, Clyde?" Mrs. Grady exclaimed, admiring the newly finished sties.

Clyde didn't answer at first. He was examining the new fences, testing them here and there for sturdiness, checking over every inch of the new roof Danny had put on Seymour's hut. Only then did he break into a smile and nod his head in approval. "It's a far sight better than I could have done, Danny—that's for sure! Never thought I'd see this old place look-

ing so distinguished—for a pigpen, that is!"
And he laughed, clapping Danny on the back.

Danny had been certain Clyde was going to
find fault with the job. Every morning he'd
come over and watch Danny work for a few
moments, then leave. "Coming along, boy.
Coming along . . ." was the most enthusiastic
he became even though Mrs. Grady seemed to
speak of nothing else. Five or six times a day
she'd come out from the store to see how
Danny was progressing, encouraging him, telling him how fine it all looked. It was odd, but
Danny began to look forward more to Clyde's
silent examinations and simple "Coming along,
boy. Coming along . . ." than to all his
mother's excitement.

"I thought maybe I could get to the barn,
too, this week, but the fencing took longer than
I expected," Danny found himself explaining.

"The barn, too!" Clyde said. "I'm surprised
you got the sties done in just a week. Ain't you,
Alice?"

"Nothing surprises me about Danny once he
puts his mind to something," she said proudly,
kissing him. "I told you that, Clyde. You've just
never seen Danny put his mind to something,
that's all."

Clyde nodded in agreement, reached into his
pocket, and pulled out a crisp, new twenty-

dollar bill. "Here, Danny, this is for you. I know if I had to pay a professional, it'd cost me ten times that. It's not much for all the hard work you done, but it's my way of saying thanks."

"Hey, that's okay, Clyde. This is great. Really. Thanks!" He hoped Clyde knew he meant it. All week he'd expected Clyde to pay him at least twenty-five dollars—the job was easily worth that. If it hadn't been for the thought of the money, Danny knew he would have given up a hundred times. But strangely he wasn't disappointed with the twenty. The money didn't seem so important now. Clyde was pleased. He understood how hard Danny had worked. Suddenly that mattered more.

"You know I'd give you more if I could, Danny," Clyde went on.

"Hey, Clyde—twenty bucks is great. I never expected that much!"

"Well, I've been thinking about something else for you. You know my .22? I don't use it much anymore. It's just sitting around gathering dust. I thought maybe you'd like it. It's over in the smokehouse now. You might want to take it into the woods and try it out. You know, see if you can hit a squirrel or rabbit just to get the feel of it."

Danny wasn't sure how to respond. He didn't

like hunting much, at least he hadn't the few times his mother had talked him into going with Clyde. It seemed Danny never did anything right. Clyde was always annoyed. Danny could never aim the old gun Clyde gave him to use, and he was always talking at the wrong time, making too much noise or walking too fast or too slowly.

"Well, what do you say, boy?" Clyde asked.

"I don't know," Danny said hesitantly. "I mean, that's your gun."

"I know that, boy!" Clyde laughed. "You think I forgot!"

"No." Danny laughed.

"Besides, when a boy's thirteen, it's time for him to have a rifle of his own. That's when I got mine. And anyway, if a father can't give his son his .22, then I don't know what!"

Danny smiled. Hunting might not be so bad if he had a .22 like that all his own. Willy had a .22, but it wasn't nearly so nice as Clyde's. "Hey, Clyde, thanks."

"Well, come on then! Let's go get it."

"And don't worry about your chores this morning," his mother added. "Your father and I will tend to them."

Clyde nodded. "You deserve a day off, Danny." And as they walked toward the smokehouse, he added, "I was just thinking—why don't I drive you over to the Fordhook trail? You can do your shooting on the mountain. It'll be pretty unwieldy carrying that rifle on your bike, and it's not much of a walk back home from the Fordhook."

"Okay, Clyde. Thanks."

Clyde grinned happily. "Well, come on, boy. Let's hustle. You want to get out there shooting just as fast as you can!"

~

Beth started up the Fordhook trail, but she didn't stay on it long. Last week she'd gone up all five trails on Mt. Ash and then forged some of her own. Forging new trails was more fun than following old ones, and with her compass she knew she wouldn't get lost. She stopped at a clearing to rest and pick some tall, blue wildflowers growing in a patch where the sunlight flooded through the trees. Sitting on a rock, she twisted the long, thin stems together into a necklace. She loved making flower necklaces. Her mother always made them out of dandelions; but these flowers made a more delicate necklace. Her mother would like it.

As she sat twisting the stems together, she remembered the bears picking berries. She'd seen them almost every day last week, always around noon time, hunting through the bushes near the caves. It was almost eleven forty-five now. She'd have to hurry if she wanted to see the bears today because they didn't stay too long—and she still had to climb to the cliff above the caves.

Sometimes Beth wished she could share the bears with her father; but she knew she couldn't. It was terrible to have something so wonderful as those bears and have to keep them a secret. *Probably nobody else in the whole world knows about them. And nobody else loves them but me. So they're my bears, my own wonderful bears!* she thought as she put on her necklace and started back to the trail.

Once she reached the steep, rocky part just below the turn-off to the caves, she stopped to examine the trail, trying to decide the surest way up amid the rocks and giant roots jutting out from the earth. It was easy to slip here and go rolling to the bottom of the incline. That was okay sometimes, but not today. She didn't have the time to waste.

As she was mapping out her route, a noise resounded through the mountain. She could feel the vibrations all about her, and it seemed what she heard was a loud, cracking snap. It came again, maybe nearby, but it was impossible for Beth to tell exactly. She became nervous, uncertain about what to do. The sounds of the mountain were usually too soft for her to hear; and besides, this sound seemed not to belong on the mountain. It was loud and startling, like the harsh sounds of the city. She looked up the trail again, and as she did, she saw a boy with a rifle running backward from the direction of the caves. It was Danny Grady.

Beth called to him. He turned to her, tripped and fell, but scrambled quickly to his feet, screaming at her, "Run!"

Beth didn't understand him, but she felt Danny's terror. His face and arms were bleeding, and his skin was a sickly green-white. She remembered the noise she'd heard and began to panic. "What's wrong?" she cried.

Grabbing her, Danny pointed up the trail. A large black bear was standing on two feet at the top of the incline. The great animal bared its teeth and roared. Saliva dripped from its mouth, and Beth's heart started pounding as the bear's rage filled her ears. Her whole body trembled. Like Danny, she began running backward, afraid to turn her back on the bear.

The bear moved amazingly fast without losing its footing. Looking at Danny, Beth knew he couldn't help her now. He was standing motionless, frozen to the ground. Beth remembered reading that some adult bears don't climb trees. Was it a black bear or a grizzly? She couldn't remember—but the bear was getting so close. In front of her was a pine tree with thick bare branches not far from the ground. It was their only escape.

"Come on," she shouted.

Danny just stared at her.

"Come on!" she screamed, tugging at his arm.

Finally Danny followed, clinging to her frantically. She ran to the tree and pulled herself up. Danny climbed after her, but the first two branches snapped under his weight. Terrified, he sat on the ground. "I can't!" he cried out.

Beth reached down for him. "Come on. You can do it. You have to!" she said, speaking slowly and clearly and as calmly as she could.

Danny turned to see the bear lumbering toward them down the trail. As he stood up again, the rifle slipped from his hand. Desperately he reached for the higher branches. Beth wondered if they'd hold. She prayed they would. If they didn't the bear would get Danny for sure.

He hoisted himself up. This time the branches held. Beth climbed higher and Danny followed, but as he did he kept pulling at her legs. She knew there was more to fear now from Danny in his panic than from the bear. She feared he would send them both tumbling to the ground.

When they were high enough to be out of the bear's reach, Beth stopped. "We're okay, now," she shouted.

The bear halted on the trail about ten feet from the tree. Beth shivered as she watched the animal bare its huge, white teeth. Its strength and fearlessness were terrifying; yet, as Beth watched it rear up and sensed its roar again, she shivered with a strange feeling of pleasure. This was her bear, the one she'd watched searching peacefully for food and playing lazily with its cub. Beth thought it had never looked so beautiful.

Suddenly the bear dropped on all fours, turned and headed back up the mountain. At the point on the trail where Beth had first seen Danny running, the bear cub was sitting, waiting for its mother.

Beth and Danny stayed in the tree long after the bears disappeared. At last Beth decided it was safe to come down. "What happened?" she asked when they reached the ground.

Danny had to take a few deep breaths before

answering. His face was flushed, and Beth noticed his hands trembling. "It was an accident. I'd been trying to shoot at some squirrels, and I left the safety catch off. I tripped. The gun went off—"

"You were shooting at the bears?" Beth demanded angrily.

"No! Didn't you understand? I said it was an accident. I was watching them and then I thought the big one saw me, so I got scared and started to back up. I tripped. The gun just went off!" he insisted. "Then I shot at it again because it was coming at me. But I missed."

Danny stooped to get Clyde's rifle. He pulled at his shirt, using it to wipe off the barrel, and anxiously checked to see that it was all right. "It's okay. Come on, we better go."

He reached out to help Beth as they made their way along the rocky incline, but she shook her head. "I'm fine," she told him.

Danny climbed down hesitantly, looking nervously back up the mountain, unable to shake the feeling that the bear was nearby. He wanted to get away from there as quickly as possible.

"Wait a minute," Beth said, turning back toward the tree. "There! See those blue flowers hanging on that branch? They're mine. I was wearing them around my neck." She reached up, but the necklace was too high. "Can you reach them?"

"I guess."

"Be careful!" Beth cried as his hand touched the flowers.

As gently as he could, Danny unhooked the necklace from the pine needles and handed it to Beth.

"Oh, thank you! Look, it's only broken in one place! I can fix it easily."

"But why do you want it? It's all wilted."

"That's okay. I'm going to take it home and press it in a book and keep it forever! So I'll always have something to remind me of today."

"Come on," Danny urged. "We gotta get out of here." As they started down the trail, Danny thought, *What does she want to remember today for? The faster I forget, the better. . . .* And then something else occurred to him: *What if she goes blabbing to everyone about how wonderful it was to be chased by a bear? What if Clyde hears? I had a gun and everything and I still ran scared. What if Willy and Brian hear? There'll be no laughing this one off. . .*

They were almost to the bottom of the mountain when Danny grabbed Beth's arm to stop her. "Hey, Beth, I was thinking. What if we keep this whole thing a secret? Just between you and me. I mean, folks might get scared if they knew about the bears. Not that people don't know we got bears here, but nobody sees them much."

Beth nodded seriously. She'd been thinking about people being scared. She didn't want her parents finding out about her bears. Especially not now.

"Want to shake on it?" Beth asked.

"Yeah! Good!"

Beth held out her hand to him.

"Now, remember," he said, "it's like a solemn pact when people shake on secrets."

"I know *that*," Beth answered, annoyed that he thought she didn't know. "I always keep my promises even if I don't shake on them."

"Good," Danny said. "Me, too."

Chapter Ten

Beth and Danny separated at the swing, but before they did Danny said, "Beth, I gotta tell you something."

"Yes."

"Well," he began nervously, "I just wanted to say thanks. I mean, if it wasn't for you, that bear might have got me."

"Oh, that's okay. But you better never go shooting after bears!"

"Don't worry about that!" He smiled, and started across the field, the rifle slung over his shoulder. *I'll tell Clyde I took a couple of shots at a rabbit or something,* he was thinking, *but I won't say I hit any.*

Danny was surprised to see Clyde's truck in the driveway. Then he remembered it was Monday. The smokehouse was closed on Mondays.

Mrs. Grady was in the kitchen when Danny came in. "Hi, Ma!" he called.

"Well, Danny, did you have a good time?" she asked, not looking up from the shopping list she was writing. "You know, your father was so happy you went off like that with his gun," she began and turned to Danny. When she saw him, she gasped, "Danny! What happened to you?"

"Nothing, Ma. Why?"

"Well, look at you. You're all cut up!"

Danny felt his face. It was scratched. Why hadn't he thought of that?

"And that awful cut on your elbow! What did you get into?"

"Nothing, Ma. I just tripped. . . ." He felt his stomach tighten.

"Tripped? Goodness sakes, Danny, you look like you fell off a cliff. These are bad. They're going to get infected if you don't clean them up. Now you tell me, did you and Willy get into some ruckus with that gun?"

"No, Ma, I swear. I tripped on the trail. You know, that part near the caves where it's real steep and all."

"Well, boy," Clyde said as he came into the kitchen, "it looks like you got caught up in something nasty."

"And he won't tell me what. He claims he tripped, but those scratches don't look like tripping to me."

"Did you get into any trouble with the gun?" Clyde asked.

Danny could feel himself panicking. He didn't know how to answer.

"Well, boy, what happened?" Clyde demanded.

As Danny looked at Clyde, his mind went blank.

"Come on, Danny. We're waiting. Is the gun all right? Did you get into something that messed up the gun, and you're afraid to tell me?"

"No, Clyde, honest. It's not that. See," he said, handing the rifle to Clyde. "The gun's fine."

Clyde took it and quickly examined the barrel and the stock. "Looks okay. Been fired, I see. What did you get?"

Danny felt sick.

"Oh, for goodness sakes, Danny. What could have happened that you can't tell us?" His mother sounded annoyed.

"Why, Alice, there's just a whole mess of things a thirteen-year-old boy can get into with a gun. Ain't that right, Danny?"

He wanted to run. He thought of how proud and happy Clyde had been this morning about the fencing. *But he won't be proud if he finds out I had to have a little deaf girl save me. What did he ever give me his gun for anyway? I wish I hadn't taken it.*

"Now, you better tell," Clyde was saying, " 'cause we're gonna find out sooner or later."

"It was a bear!" Danny blurted out.

"A bear!" Clyde laughed. "If a bear came close enough to scratch you up like that, you wouldn't have much left of you, boy."

"The bear didn't scratch me!" Danny insisted. He couldn't think of what to say next.

"Well, come on, boy." Clyde laughed again. "Something must have happened, and this time the story better be more likely than a bear!"

"Well, see . . . I was out in the woods—looking for squirrels like you said. I just wanted to try the gun, Clyde."

"Did you and Willy get into something, boy?"

"No. I swear. I was all by myself. . . ."

106

"And a bear attacked?" Clyde asked sarcastically.

"Let him speak, Clyde," Mrs. Grady said.

"I'm only trying to get at the truth," Clyde insisted, staring at Danny.

"See, I was out in the woods, walking around. I'd shot at one squirrel and missed. I was just walking . . . and I heard this screaming. I went to investigate, and I saw that little deaf kid, Beth . . ." Danny stopped. He hadn't planned to say that. He hadn't planned to break his promise. It just came out, and now he couldn't stop himself. "She was running and screaming, and a big mother bear was after her. I shot at it a couple of times, but it kept on coming. Finally I grabbed Beth and ran. But she was so scared she fell and I fell with her. We rolled down this real rocky part of the trail, and that's how I got cut, I guess."

"Well, what happened then?" Clyde urged him on. "How'd you get away?"

"We climbed a tree," he said quickly. "I lifted Beth up on a branch, and she got the idea. We stayed there until the bear went away. Maybe I got scratched there, too."

"Is Beth all right?" Mrs. Grady asked.

"She's okay."

"Did you bring her home?"

Danny nodded. "I just left her at the swing."

"Why didn't you tell me, Danny?" his mother asked.

"I was afraid you'd get all upset about the bear."

"Well, it is upsetting, thinking there's a mad bear so close to town," Mrs. Grady sighed, looking at her husband. "I think I'll call Beth's mother. It must have been a terrible fright for that poor child."

"No, Ma. Don't do that!"

"Well, why not, Danny? It's the least I can do as a neighbor."

"I don't know," he said uneasily. "It might seem like you're bragging or something, 'cause of me helping Beth and all."

"Oh, don't be silly, Danny. I'm not going to brag. I simply want to find out how the child is."

"But I told you, she's okay."

Clyde put his arm around Danny. "Nobody's talking about bragging, boy. Now you go ahead and call, Alice."

"I'm gonna clean up," Danny said, following his mother from the kitchen.

Clyde quickly caught up with him. "You know, that was a brave thing, Danny, plain and simple. You should be feeling mighty proud."

"I guess," Danny shrugged.

"Then what are you so downcast about? That's no way for a hero to act."

"Oh, Clyde, I'm no hero."

Ignoring Danny's protest, Clyde said, "I know what the problem is: I bet you're sore 'cause that bear got away. But don't be. It ain't easy to shoot a bear—not when she's tearing at you."

Just tell him. Tell him the truth and get it over.

Clyde went on. "And not with a .22. You need a much more powerful gun if you want to do more than scratch a bear. But if you had the right weapon, and you ever got another chance at that bear—pow! You could get her easy!"

"You think so?" he asked uncertainly.

"Of course you could. I wasn't always the hunter I am, either. Why, when I was your age I couldn't handle a gun nowhere near as well as you."

Now's the time to tell him. Tell him now! But when he looked up and saw Clyde grinning so proudly, looking so happy, the words wouldn't come out of his mouth.

"You know something, boy?" Clyde asked, putting his hand on Danny's shoulder. "I'm proud of you. I truly am. Ain't everyone who can keep a cool head in a dangerous situation."

Just then Mrs. Grady came back. "Well, I feel better having called. Carol said Beth was fine, and she thanked me for calling."

"Did she say anything else?" Danny asked nervously.

"No, but she sounded a little queer. At first I didn't even think she knew what I was talking about. But I suppose she must have been pretty upset over the whole thing, Beth being deaf and all. Clyde, you almost ready to go?"

"All set," he answered and, turning to Danny, he explained: "Seems there's all kinds of big sales going on in Montpelier, and your Ma thinks I need some new clothes for your cousin Barbara's wedding. Well, maybe she's right. The suit I got married in don't even close! I guess it's less painful buying a new one than going on a diet!"

Danny laughed with him. "Have a good time," he said.

"Oh, and you clean up your rifle," Clyde added as he opened the door. "First rule of owning a rifle—always keep it clean."

"I will."

"Clean yourself up first," his mother reminded him. "And there's ham and some cole slaw in the refrigerator."

Clyde held the door open for Mrs. Grady,

and when she was outside, he turned again to Danny. "Ain't it lucky I gave you that gun today, boy? I hate to think of what would have happened to that little girl if I hadn't."

Danny nodded, but inside he shivered. As he watched Clyde leave he thought, *How could I have ever thought of telling him the truth? I can't now. Not ever.*

Chapter Eleven

Beth was playing cards with her father. She didn't notice her mother next to her until she felt the cards being grabbed out of her hands.

"Do you know who just called?" Mrs. Hampton demanded anxiously.

Beth shook her head.

"Alice Grady."

"Well, what did she say that's gotten you so upset?" Mr. Hampton asked.

"Tell him, Beth," her mother ordered.

Beth couldn't speak. She couldn't believe

Danny had told about the bears. They'd made a pact! They'd shaken hands on it.

"Will somebody tell me what's going on?" Mr. Hampton asked.

"Alice called to find out how Beth was," Mrs. Hampton began as she sat down on the couch across from Beth. Beth watched her mother's lips very closely. "Apparently Beth was chased by a bear when she was on the mountain today, but she didn't think that was important enough to tell us. If Danny hadn't heard her screaming—" Mrs. Hampton stopped, shaking her head. "Oh, Ben, God knows what could have happened to her. I told you it wasn't safe for her on the mountain alone. I told you."

"But that's not true!" Beth cried out. "Danny couldn't have said that."

"Why not?" her mother demanded.

She couldn't tell them about the pact. Instead she insisted, "Because it's not true! Danny didn't save me. I saved him. I was walking up the trail near the turn-off to the caves, and all of a sudden I saw Danny. The bear was after *him!*"

"Why didn't you tell us this before?" her father asked.

"I don't know . . . I'm sorry. . . ."

Her mother wrung her hands in dismay. "Ben, as far as I'm concerned, this whole mountain affair is off."

"No!"

"I'm afraid I have to agree with your mother."

"You can't, Daddy! I can take care of myself—it was *my* idea to climb a tree. Danny was so scared he didn't know what to do. If we hadn't climbed the tree, the bear would have gotten us for sure!"

Her father put his arm around Beth, trying to calm her. "I believe you, Beth. I'm proud you had enough sense to act as quickly as you did. But that doesn't change the fact that you deliberately kept what happened from us."

"But I'm sorry! I am! I'll never do it again!"

Mrs. Hampton took her hand. "It isn't just a matter of being sorry," she said firmly. "The mountain isn't a safe place for you. . . . Ben, she simply can't go up there alone."

"No!" Turning to her father, Beth pleaded, "Not for the whole summer?"

"We'll see."

"It's not fair!" she cried, pulling at his arm. "It's not fair. You can't stop me! You can't!"

Her father sadly shook his head.

"Please, Daddy!"

Mrs. Hampton tapped her. "The answer is

'no'. And no amount of carrying on is going to change it. You were chased by a bear! I can't believe you even want to go back!"

"But it's not the bear's fault! Danny was shooting at her. The bear had to protect her baby."

"Don't you see, Beth? The reason doesn't matter. Not when you're deaf," her mother said. "Next time the danger could come from something you can't hear."

"Not on the mountain!"

"There's nothing more to discuss," her mother told her.

"I hate you! I hate everyone!" She ran toward the front door.

Her mother quickly caught up with her, grabbing her by the arm to turn her around. "Where are you going?" she demanded.

"Leave me alone!"

"Don't talk to me that way!"

"I'm going to the swing! Is that okay?"

"No. You're going to your room. I'm not putting up with this kind of behavior."

"Let her go," Mr. Hampton said. "She's upset."

"She's always upset."

"Come on, Carol. Going on the mountain was important to her."

"Oh, all right." Mrs. Hampton thought for a

moment, then sighed. "But I don't like to see her like this."

Beth didn't answer. She ran out the front door toward the field, but even as she did, she knew she wasn't going to the swing. She was going to Danny's house. *I'll get him for this! I'll get him!* she promised herself. She didn't know how. And she didn't care. She kept on running.

When Beth reached the Gradys', she peered in through the kitchen door, and when she saw nobody inside, she raced around to the front and rang the bell. After waiting a few seconds, she rang again. Still nobody answered. *They've probably gone out,* she thought angrily, and was about to ring the bell one more time, when the door opened.

"Beth!" Danny gasped.

"We had a pact!" she burst out. "We shook on it! And you broke it!"

"I'm . . . I'm sorry . . ." he began, but he was too confused to say anything else. He never expected Beth to confront him like this.

"And I got punished because of it!"

"But why? You didn't do anything wrong."

"Because my parents are scared of the bears, and now they won't let me go on the mountain alone." She spoke slowly and clearly. She wanted to make sure Danny understood her. "That's why I made the pact with you! I didn't want them to know! I hate you, Danny. I want you to know that." She felt like kicking him. She would have if she wasn't wearing sandals; but she couldn't kick hard enough with sandals. Instead she told him, "I think you're the most disgusting person in the world!"

"Look, Beth, I'm really sorry you got in trouble. . . ."

"Stop saying you're sorry!"

"Then what do you want?" he asked nervously, because if she wanted him to admit he was wrong to her parents and Clyde—well, he was sorry, but he couldn't do that. There was no way he could do that now.

She thought for a moment. What did she want? Danny couldn't do anything to change her parents' minds. Even if he told the truth, it wouldn't matter. They still wouldn't let her on the mountain alone. That was what she wanted, the only thing she wanted, and Danny couldn't give that to her. No, she hadn't come to get anything from him—she'd come to get him back, to make him suffer, too. But as she glared angrily at him, she realized she couldn't even do that. Kicking him, punching him, screaming at him— things like that didn't hurt or matter, not the way the loss of the mountain and the bears mattered.

"I wish you were dead! I wish the bear had killed you!" She turned and ran back through the field.

Beth jumped on the swing and began pumping furiously. Tears of anger and frustration streamed off her face as she flew faster and faster. *Danny lies, and I get punished. Nothing happens to him! Only me! It's not fair. They can't stop me from going on the mountain all summer. They can't. I watched the bears every day last week and nothing happened. Nothing would ever have happened—if it wasn't for Danny!*

As she cried she pumped harder and harder, beating the air with her legs until they ached. Finally she let the swing come slowly to a stop, sitting motionless. *They're just being stupid and dumb because they're scared of the bears. They're blaming the bears for chasing Danny. But it's his fault. Everything is his fault. He promised he wouldn't tell. He promised! It's just not fair. . . .*

"Do you think it's fair, Mr. Oak?" she asked. "Do you?"

Suddenly she kicked the ground with her feet, making the swing jerk sideways. Then she jumped up and shouted, "I hate you, Danny Grady! I hate you all!" And she started home.

When she reached the tall grass, she saw her mother heading toward her.

What does she want? Beth moaned.

"Are you feeling any better?" Mrs. Hampton asked when they met.

"No. Why should I?"

"Well, I have something that might help you cheer up."

"Nothing will ever make me happy. Ever again! Going on the mountain is the best thing in the world. And so are the bears! I love them. I know they wouldn't hurt me. I know it!"

Mrs. Hampton frowned. "I didn't come out here to argue with you over that. And besides, we didn't say you could never go up again. Just not alone. Anyway, Mrs. Clarke called. She invited you over to the farm tomorrow morning. I thought you'd want to go, so I said 'yes'."

Beth sighed.

"Don't you want to go?"

"I guess . . ."

"I bet you can go over there a lot. Like last summer."

"But it's not the same as going on the mountain."

"No, it's not the same, but you can have just as much fun."

Oh, shut up! Beth felt like screaming. *You*

*don't know about the mountain or my bears. You
don't know about anything like that. Nothing is more
fun than that!* But she couldn't say that, so she
shrugged and said, "I guess . . ."

~

"Danny, you up there?" Danny heard his
mother call.

"Yeah," Danny answered.

"Well, come on down. There's a whole bunch
of things to be unloaded from the truck."

Clyde was trying to maneuver some two-by-
fours from the truck when Danny got there.
"What's that for?" Danny asked.

"For a new barn door! Grab some, will you?
Let's just lean them against the truck here.
We'll bring it over to the barn later."

"A new barn door?" Danny asked doubtfully.
"I'm not sure I can build a door, Clyde."

Clyde laughed. "I was thinking maybe we
could do it together. Doors are kind of tricky;
but I've done a few myself. It's the stalls that
are a real mess. They need a lot of work, but all
we gotta do is work on one right now."

"One?" Danny asked. Clyde wasn't making
sense.

"Well, I don't think I could see my way clear
to buying more than one horse. Nor for a while
anyway."

"A horse?"

"You got anything against horses?"

"No. Nothing. I just never thought of getting one."

"Would you like to?"

"Well, sure . . ."

Clyde smiled. "I thought as much. The truth is, I've been wanting a horse for a while, but with the hogs and the smokehouse and all— well, I've never thought I'd have the time. But you and me working together—it wouldn't be so bad. It's been my experience that the pleasure of a horse is worth all the work—seeing, of course, you want to take on a project like the barn."

Danny thought for a moment and said, "I could get started tomorrow."

"Not tomorrow," Clyde said seriously. "I've been giving that bear some thought. You know, it ain't right for a bear to attack like that. I'm worried. Stopped in town on the way home and talked to Fred McCowan and Bob Willard and some others. We're gonna go after that bear tomorrow morning in an organized way. No telling who or when she'll attack next time if we don't get her first."

Danny felt a sick feeling in the pit of his stomach."I—I don't understand, Clyde."

"Look, boy, there's a crazed bear on the loose. What's not to understand about that? Soon as we finish unloading here, I'm gonna make some calls, and see if we can get some more men to come. Once word spreads about what happened to you and Beth, I bet we get ten, maybe fifteen men."

"But isn't it hard to find the bear? I mean, nobody hardly ever sees bears around here."

" 'Course it's hard, boy. But that's what hunting's all about. There's always a chance we won't find her. But I don't know—I got a feeling we will. And if we do, Danny, I'm gonna hand my gun over to you and give you another chance at her. Now come on, let's get this truck unloaded."

Danny stood staring after Clyde, the sick feeling in his stomach growing worse. "A bear hunt!" he gasped, kicking a tire. Angrily, he reached into the truck and grabbed a grocery bag, jerking it toward him; and as he did, the bag ripped and oranges and cans of frozen juice spilled out. "Oh, great!" he cried, stuffing the oranges into another bag. *I should have told Clyde before. I should have told him I lied! But I can't now. Stupid! I'm so stupid! What did I think— that he was going to keep the bear a secret?*

"Danny," Clyde called from the house, "you

finish unloading. I'm gonna start making some calls."

"Clyde? Maybe you shouldn't. . . ."

"Well, why not? There ain't much time before tomorrow."

"Yeah, I know. I was just thinking—it looks like rain, and the wood shouldn't get wet."

"This ain't gonna take long. We'll get the wood inside soon enough." And he disappeared to make the phone calls. There was no stopping the hunt now.

Danny started for the house. His eye caught sight of the wood leaning against the truck, and he laughed bitterly. *One thing for sure—if Clyde finds out the truth, he won't want to fix up the barn and get a horse with me.*

Chapter Twelve

The Clarkes' dog, a big collie named Lady, barked wildly when the Hamptons' car pulled into the driveway at six-thirty the next morning.

"Hi, Lady!" Beth called as she climbed out. Lady leaped up on her, licking her face. Beth turned to her father. "She remembers me!"

"I think so!"

Lady's barking brought Jamie out of the house. "Mommy, Beth's here!" he shouted.

Mrs. Clarke came to the door, carrying a baby. "Good morning," she greeted them.

"How have you been?" Mr. Hampton asked.

"Fine, but tired. This is such a busy time of year."

He nodded. "The baby's getting big."

"He's quite a load."

"Well, I'll let you go then. I told Beth I'd pick her up about ten or ten-thirty."

"That's fine. Any time."

Mr. Hampton honked the horn, and Beth turned around. "Bye, Daddy!" She waved, then looked back at Mrs. Clarke.

Mrs. Clarke smiled. "If you two want to help with the milking, you'd better hurry to the barn. Then you come to the house later, Beth, and we'll have a nice long chat."

Jamie grabbed Beth's hand. "Come on. I'll show you the calves." Realizing he'd spoken with his head turned away from Beth, he faced her and said again, "Come on. I'll show you the calves."

"Well, here are my helpers!" Mr. Clarke smiled happily when he saw Beth and Jamie, making Beth feel at home. He handed her an old pair of high rubber boots, and after she pulled them on, she followed Jamie into the barn. It was dark and damp inside and smelled of cow dung. Even the walls seemed to be made of the wet, heavy, smelly stuff. Beth held her breath as she walked alongside Jamie, her feet squishing in the mud of the barn floor. Gradually her eyes grew accustomed to the dark and her nose to the smell.

Red, the hired man, waved when he saw her, and hurried over. "I hear you and Danny Grady had a run-in with a bear yesterday," he said.

"How do you know?" Beth asked.

"Everyone in town knows by now. Clyde's organizing a bear hunt."

"A bear hunt!" Beth cried. The thought of it sent shock waves through her body.

Red nodded. "Ten o'clock this morning. Gonna go up the Fordhook trail to the caves. That's where you seen them, right?"

Beth couldn't answer. She was desperately trying to make sense of what Red had said: her bears, her beautiful bears, were going to be hunted—all because of Danny's lie! "But it's not true!" she cried suddenly, turning to Mr. Clarke. "The bear was only trying to protect its baby. Danny lied!" Her words tumbled out too quickly.

"Didn't catch what you said, Beth," Mr. Clarke told her.

Again she explained about Danny.

Red tapped her. "It don't follow. Clyde said the bear just took after you."

"But Danny lied. The bear was only trying to protect its baby! She didn't hurt anyone. The bears should be free. You can't hurt them! They belong to the mountain!"

Mr. Clarke and Red exchanged glances. "Guess we have a nature lover here," Red teased.

Beth felt herself growing hot from embarrassment and anger. She hated to be made fun of, especially about something so important as the bears.

"I don't think the bears should be hunted either!" Jamie announced suddenly, grabbing Beth's hand.

Beth looked at Jamie. She hadn't understood him but from the way he held her hand, she knew he was on her side. That was nice, but it wasn't enough. What could she and Jamie do to stop a bear hunt?

Mr. Clarke smiled sadly. "The bears seem mighty important to you," he said.

She nodded.

Jamie pulled at his father's arm. "I don't want the bears to be hunted. You do something, Daddy."

When Mr. Clarke didn't answer right away, Beth felt hopeful. Maybe he could do something after all. . . .

Finally Mr. Clarke shook his head. "I'm

sorry. I can't do anything. Besides, I'm not so sure anything should be done. It's not safe with a bear like that around."

Of course it's safe! she wanted to yell. But that wouldn't make Mr. Clarke or Red or anyone change their minds. They believed Danny's story. They wanted to kill her bears. *But I won't let them!* she decided.

"Well, come on. We better get these cows moving. They're just aching to be milked," Mr. Clarke said.

Without thinking, Beth said, "I can't stay now."

Jamie pulled at her arm. "But why? I haven't even shown you the calves."

"I'll be back soon. I just thought of something very important I forgot to do. It won't take long."

"Is it because of the bears? Did I upset you?" Mr. Clarke asked.

"Oh, no! It's just something I forgot. I'll be back in a while. . . ." And she ran back across the barn, pulled off the rubber boots, and started across the meadow. She didn't want to pass by the farmhouse now. She didn't want Mrs. Clarke to see her leaving.

~

It was a long way from the farm to Mt. Ash; but Beth wasn't worried. She had plenty of

time. It wasn't even seven and the hunt
wouldn't start until ten. She'd be back at the
farm by then, and everything would be all
right. She knew it. She felt it. All she had to do
was search around the caves for the bears.
They had to be nearby. They came there ev-
eryday. She would find them and warn them
about the hunters. She would make them leave.
She didn't know how, but she knew when she
found them, she would figure out a way.

Beth was exhausted by the time she reached
the caves. The walk to the mountain had taken
much longer than she figured. Then she had to
take the steep trail up the north side, go all the
way to the top to meet the Fordhook trail and
hike down. But now as she stood looking at the
caves, she knew it was worth it.

Pausing at a safe distance, she tried to figure
out the best way to approach the caves in case
the bears were inside. What would she do if
they were? How would she lure them out?
What if the mother bear came lunging after
her? How would she protect herself? She
thought for a moment and decided she would
just have to keep alert and move slowly and
carefully. If the bears were inside and if they
came at her, she would run as fast as she could,
leading them away from the hunters.

She was trembling as she neared the entrance to the first cave. But the sun broke through the clouds and flooded the inside with light; as she looked in, it was easy to see the bears weren't there. She peered into the other two caves. They were empty, too. She breathed a sigh of relief, then panicked. If the bears weren't in the caves, where were they? There wasn't much time left.

Frantically Beth raced through the woods searching for the bears, thinking she would find them around the next turn, behind the next bush. She forgot about the time and getting back to the farm—she forgot about everything except finding the bears. She climbed to the top of a huge rock and looked as far as she could see, but still there was no sign of the bears. Desperate now, she screamed, "Bears! Bears! Where are you? Bears, this is me, Beth. Remember me? You chased me with that boy. Can you hear me now? Go away! The hunters are coming. They want to kill you. Go away now!" She knew her words were becoming garbled, but she didn't care. The bears wouldn't care, either. They would understand her if they could only hear her. And they had to hear her. They had to.

Closing her eyes, she crossed her fingers and concentrated as hard as she could on the bears. She could see them in her mind but she couldn't picture where on the mountain they were. *Go away, bears. Listen to me. This is Beth. I'm telling you to leave Mt. Ash before they kill you,* she pleaded in silent, frenzied despair.

She was so tired. Her knees were beginning to shake, and she was about to cry. Clenching her fists tightly, trying to hold back the tears, she pleaded one last time: "Oh, bears, please go away. Go far far away."

When she looked at her watch, it was almost ten-thirty! How could she have forgotten the time? Her father was probably at the Clarkes' already. She'd be in trouble, real bad trouble. But she couldn't think about that now because it didn't really matter. Nothing mattered if she couldn't find the bears. She ran back to the trail to search the caves one more time.

~

"Daddy!" she cried out and trembled. Maybe she was seeing things. It couldn't be her father hurrying along the trail toward her. How did he know where she was? He looked angry, as angry as she'd ever seen him.

"What are you doing here?" he demanded. "Why did you leave the Clarkes' without saying where you were going? Red told you there was going to be a hunt! Why did you come here? Your mother is worried sick!"

Frightened and confused, Beth tried to think

of an answer; but she saw something more terrifying than her father's anger. Clyde Grady
followed by Danny and the other hunters.
There were so many of them. How could her
bears ever escape? Beth looked at the men; she
knew them all. There was Mr. Willard, Mr. Mc-
Cowan, Mr. Thompson, Red and other men
from town, men she liked. And there with their
fathers were Willy and Brian. She could hardly
believe they were all here—guns slung over
their shoulders, ready to kill the bears.

Instinctively, Danny began edging away from
Clyde. *What is she doing here?* But he knew the
answer: she'd come to accuse him of lying, to
call him out in front of Clyde and Willy and all
the other men. Danny wanted to run, to hide,
to disappear; but he couldn't. Beth was running
toward him, shouting, "The bears aren't here!
I searched the caves! The bears aren't here!"

Mr. Hampton ran after her and grabbed
her, turning her around. "You shouldn't have
done that!"

She pulled away from him, humiliated by
being treated like a child, and ran to Danny.
"Liar!" she burst out.

Danny turned pale.

Clyde hurried over. "What's this all about?"

"He lied!" Beth said, pointing an accusing

finger at Danny. "It wasn't like he said. He didn't save me from the bears. The bear was chasing him 'cause he tripped and his gun went off. He was so scared he didn't know what to do, and I found a tree we could climb. I saved Danny. The bear wouldn't have ever chased him if his gun hadn't gone off!"

Clyde looked at Danny, and when their eyes met, Danny blurted out, "No, Clyde! I swear."

"You're lying!" Beth insisted, stamping the earth.

Clyde turned from Beth to her father and said, "I don't understand what she wants, Ben. What's she doing up here anyway? If she wanted to accuse Danny of lying, why'd she wait till now?"

"I want you to stop the hunt!" Beth demanded before her father could answer.

"But why?" Clyde asked in bewilderment. "Those bears are dangerous. You ought to know that."

"No, they're not! They haven't hurt anyone. They belong to the mountain. You can't kill them!"

"But, Beth, those bears went after you and Danny—if they did it once, they can do it again. And next time the person might not get away."

"But they won't. They won't if they're left alone!"

"Well, maybe—but maybe not. And I sure don't think we can gamble on a thing like that. Now, Ben, I think you better get her out of here."

"Not so fast, Clyde. Why didn't you tell me about his hunt before?" Mr. Hampton demanded suddenly.

Clyde shook his head thoughtfully and then smiled, a little embarrassed. "Well, I know you ain't interested in hunting. And besides, this is a local matter."

"A local matter! Don't I live here?"

"Now don't go getting all upset, Ben. Of course, you live here, but only for the summer. And . . ."

"And nothing, Clyde! My daughter was chased by that bear, too. You should have told me what you were planning. And if you had, I would have told you Beth's story then and there. . . ."

All this talk seemed unimportant to Beth now. Only saving the bears mattered, and only Danny could do that by telling the truth. She turned to him and demanded, "Tell them you're lying, Danny! Tell them the truth!"

"He did already," Clyde spoke up quickly.

"Now maybe you're just letting your imagination get out of hand, Beth, 'cause you want to save the bears so much."

"Are you calling my daughter a liar, Clyde?" Mr. Hampton demanded angrily.

"No, of course not, Ben. I'm just saying her imagination might be playing tricks on her."

"It's not. Danny's lying," Beth cried out.

"If Beth says she's telling the truth, then she's telling the truth," Mr. Hampton said.

"Okay, Ben. Then one of these kids is lying. But who are we supposed to believe? You say your daughter's not a liar, and I'm telling you my son ain't either. But I'll say one thing—it's easier to accept the word of some pretty little deaf girl than it is of a big, strong thirteen-year-old boy."

"I don't like what you're implying, Clyde."

"I'm not implying nothing, Ben."

"We don't ask for and we don't expect any special consideration for Beth because she's deaf. But I'm telling you this girl is no liar."

"Listen here, Ben, I didn't come up here to get into a fight with you. I came here to hunt down a killer bear. Now I'm sorry I didn't tell you about the hunt. But nothing's changed as far as I can see. Nothing. And I don't see the point in us arguing about it anymore. There's a bear out there that chased my son and your daughter. I want to get it before it goes after someone else and maybe kills. There's nothing wrong with that, Ben, is there?"

The two men stood staring at each other for a few moments. Finally Mr. Hampton turned to Beth and said, "Let's go."

Beth looked from her father to Clyde and then to the other men. Nobody spoke up for her or her father—they all agreed with Clyde. She turned to Danny. Little beads of perspiration were forming on his forehead and above his lips. His fingers were wrapped so tightly around the rifle, his knuckles were white. She knew he was scared and she shouted boldly, "You said you wouldn't tell. You promised. We shook on it. We made a pact, Danny—but you broke it. And you lied! You lied, and you know it. You lied!"

Most of Beth's words were slurred and hard to understand, but the meaning was clear. Danny knew there was nothing he could say to answer her now, so he looked down at the ground and said nothing.

"Well, what are we standing around here for?" Clyde's voice suddenly boomed through the silent air. "Are we on a hunt or what?" And without waiting for a response, Clyde put his arm around Danny. "Come on, boy. We got a bear to track down."

As the men began following Clyde and Danny, Mr. Hampton took Beth's hand. "I'm sorry," he said.

Beth nodded. "Let's go," she said. She wanted to get away from there as fast as she could.

Chapter Thirteen

Neither Beth nor her father spoke as they walked down the mountain. She couldn't think of anything to say to him. She hadn't stopped the bear hunt. She hated Danny Grady. He was worse than a liar—he was a murderer. But at least her father had stood up for her. At least they had tried. Trying and losing was better than losing and not trying at all. But losing wasn't winning. Losing was awful.

Beth's eyes burned with tears. She wanted to hold on to her father tightly and squeeze him until she had no more strength. She wanted to curl up in a little ball on her bed and pull the covers over her eyes forever. . . .

The car was parked across from the trail. Beth climbed in the front seat, rolled down the window, and stared up at the mountain. Her bears were up there—somewhere. . . .

She felt her father open the other door and sit next to her; but she didn't move until she felt his hand gently resting on her. "I'm sorry, Daddy. I'm sorry," she cried at last, burying her head against him. He held her tightly. When she looked up at him, she said, "I know I was wrong. But I had to try to save the bears. I had to try."

"I know."

"Aren't you angry?"

"No. I was very proud of you up there, Beth. Despite all the odds, you did stand up for what you believed. There aren't many grown-up people who would have done what you just did."

"Aren't you going to punish me?"

"For what?"

"But I wasn't supposed to be on the mountain."

Smiling, his eyes filling with tears, he said, "How else could you have tried to save the bears if you didn't go on the mountain? Invite them to tea?"

Beth hugged her father. "I love you."

~

"Let's check out the caves first," Clyde told the hunters.

Danny stayed close to Clyde. He could hear Willy and Brian just a little way behind him, laughing and jeering, saying things like "Danny and the dummy or how Danny the Dodo was saved by the dummy!"

Danny tried to close his ears to Willy and Brian, but it was hard. They were talking loudly, loud enough for everyone to hear.

"Ignore them, boy. They'll get bored soon if you just ignore them. Besides, you're gonna do something that's gonna shut their mouths for good," he added as they neared the caves. "See, I want you to go in and check out those caves yourself. You show 'em!"

"But what if the bears are in there?"

"Don't worry, boy. The sun's shining right in them so you'll be able to see without too much problem. Besides, I'll be here watching you every minute, my gun ready."

The thought of seeing that big bear come charging at him again made Danny break out into a cold sweat. Even Willy and Brian were better than the bear, safer anyway. "Clyde, I can't," he pleaded.

"Danny, I want you to."

"But you don't know what it's like. . . ."

"Look, we ain't got time to stand here and argue, boy. You want Willy and Brian razzing you for the rest of your life about what Beth said? You gotta show 'em you're not scared."

"But I am scared," he blurted out.

"Danny, now I'm telling you to go in and search out those caves. That's all there is about it." And motioning for the others to stop, Clyde announced, "Danny's gonna check out the caves!"

"Wowee! Now ain't that brave?" Willy taunted.

"Here, you take my rifle instead," Clyde said, handing Danny his more powerful gun. "Take the safety off," he reminded him.

Danny fumbled nervously with the rifle.

"Now, go on, boy," Clyde whispered. "And remember, I won't be far behind you."

Danny wanted to throw the gun at Clyde and say "You do it!" but he slowly made his way toward the caves. As he did, the terrifying vision of the bear standing on its hind legs, roaring, baring its huge white teeth, came to him. *I hate you, Clyde,* his mind screamed, as if to blot out the memory of the bear. *I hate you for making me do this! I'm not your son. I can't be. I don't want to be!*

~

"Where did you find her, Ben?" Mrs. Hampton cried out when Beth and her father came home.

"Near the caves. It was just as I thought. She was trying to do something about the bears."

"Near the caves. Oh, my God, Ben!" she exclaimed, and looked at Beth. Her mother seemed sad and frightened but not angry. Sitting down on a chair she began to cry.

Beth could have understood her mother's anger, her screaming. She would have understood if her mother had hit her. But she couldn't understand her mother's tears; and yet Beth was moved by them. Putting her arms around her mother, she asked, "What's the matter, Mom? Why are you crying?"

Mrs. Hampton shook her head slowly, biting her lip to keep from crying. "I was so worried about you, darling. Between the hunters and the bears, I thought . . ." She couldn't go on. She didn't have to. Beth understood. She had felt the same for the bears.

"I'm sorry, Mom. I was so worried about the bears. I didn't mean to scare you. I didn't think. I just wanted to save the bears."

Mrs. Hampton took Beth on her lap and held her tightly.

"I tried to save them," Beth explained. "I had to try."

Mr. Hampton described how Beth spoke against Danny, how she tried desperately to stop the hunt. "I'm sorry, too, Beth," her mother said at last. "I didn't know how much the bears meant to you."

Mrs. Hampton made lunch, but Beth wasn't hungry. She couldn't think of food. She couldn't think of anything but the bears. She went to her room and sat on her bed, looking out the window at the mountain.

If only I could hear, she thought. *But what would I hear? The sounds of guns? Maybe. How terrible. I don't want to hear that ever. Ever. I don't want that: hearing the guns; knowing my bears are being shot, killed.* She pulled off her hearing aid and threw it on the floor. Putting her hands over her ears, she cried aloud, "I'm glad I'm deaf. I'll never have to know if my bears are dead. I'll close my eyes if anyone tries to tell me about them. I'll pretend they've gotten away. I'll pretend they escaped to Canada. I'll stay in my room all summer. Or maybe I'll go to the swing—if only I can get rid of Danny—and wait for the summer to end. I'll be happy to get back to the city. There aren't any bears to care about in the city. It's easier not to care. I hate caring. I don't ever want to care about anything ever again."

~

"Well, now, ain't you brave," Willy jeered as soon as Danny came out of the last cave. "Ain't he brave, Brian? Searching out those caves?"

"Brave as the little dummy!" Brian laughed.

"That's why he was so brave. He knew the dummy was telling the truth when she said the bears weren't in the caves. He knew it because he knew the dummy don't lie. But we all know that now."

Clyde was at Danny's side in a moment, whispering, "You gotta defend yourself, boy. If you don't, everybody's gonna believe Beth's story."

"What would you have done if you'd seen the bear, Danny?" Willy taunted. "Cry for the dummy to come help?"

Danny felt the world was closing in on him.

"Come on, boy," Clyde whispered, impatiently now.

Leave me alone! Danny screamed inside, looking from Willy to Clyde—Willy laughing, Clyde pushing. . . .

It was Mr. Thompson, Hank's father, who came to Danny's defense. "Okay, Willy, that's enough. We're hunting a bear. If you don't know how to behave, then you'll have to leave."

"I'll be the one who decides that," Willy's father spoke up. "Seems to me something strange is going on here if what that little deaf girl said is true."

"But it's not true, Frank," Clyde snapped. "Danny's already said so."

"No, Clyde. You were the one who said it," Mr. Donaldson reminded him.

"Yeah, well, let's hear the yellow-bellied chicken say it!" Willy demanded.

Clyde's fingers dug into his shoulder. "Go on, boy. Make your stand."

"I'm no more scared of a bear than you, Willy!" Danny heard himself yelling.

Willy laughed. "That'll be the day, Danny boy! I sure wouldn't let some dummy girl help me escape!"

"Go on, Danny!" Clyde ordered.

I'm going! I'm going! Danny answered; but it was only in his mind and he didn't move. He saw Mr. Thompson walking toward him, smiling, talking gently as he always did. "Take it easy, Danny. Anyone with any sense is rightly scared of a bear."

Right, Mr. Thompson. Right. But you're Dad's friend. And Dad's not here anymore. Dad's dead. Clyde's here, don't you see. Clyde's here. . . .

"Now, boy!" He felt Clyde shoving him toward Willy the same way he'd taken his hand with the knife and shoved it into the cow's belly.

Danny lunged at Willy, and the two of them began punching each other furiously. Each time Willy hit him, a pain burst inside Danny with such fury that he wanted to beat Willy until he couldn't move anymore. He wanted to beat Willy for teaming up with Brian against him. He wanted to beat Willy for every time Willy laughed at him. . . . And all the while, he could hear Clyde calling his name, cheering him on. Pushing him. Pushing him. *If it hadn't been for Clyde, none of this would have happened. It was Clyde who made me lie . . . Clyde who called the hunt . . . Clyde who made me fight Willy.*

With each new burst of pain from Willy's fists, Danny's old hatred of Clyde exploded within him. *It's Clyde I should be hitting . . . Clyde, who made me slaughter that cow . . . Clyde, who's taken my father's place!*

Danny felt two hands on his back, pulling at him, trying to get him off Willy, and suddenly the smell of the smokehouse was all around him. The hands were Clyde's. He knew it. Without thinking, Danny jumped off Willy and turned on Clyde, hitting him as he'd hit Willy.

He thought he heard Clyde's voice yelling something at him, but he couldn't make it out. He couldn't make out Clyde clearly. There were tears or streaks of sweat or maybe it was blood covering his eyes, blurring his vision.

Then he felt Clyde's hand gripping his shoulder, shaking him, trying to get him to stop. He wouldn't stop. Nothing could stop him. With one desperate move, he pulled free of Clyde's grip. He heard a wild, animal-like screech coming from somewhere inside him as he plunged at Clyde again. Then he felt Clyde's hand hitting the side of his face with such force he fell back on the ground. His ears were ringing. He thought he was going to pass out.

He didn't pass out. He lay on the ground, gasping for breath. Every muscle and bone in his body ached now. His ears were still ringing, and his eyes were wet. He tried to get up but he couldn't move, and he settled back on the ground. . . . Maybe he passed out. He didn't know. The next thing he knew was Clyde's voice.

"What came over you, boy? You acted like a madman. I thought you were gonna kill Willy and me. What came over you?"

Danny opened his eyes, but he still couldn't

see well. He pulled up his shirt and wiped his eyes with it. The shirt was stained with blood, and there was a throbbing from above his right eye. He sat up and his vision grew clearer. Everyone was looking down at him. He could see Willy's eye was beginning to swell and his lower lip was already swollen. His face was covered with dirt. Danny wanted to laugh, but his jaw hurt too much.

"This is a hell of a thing. We come here for a bear hunt, and we practically kill ourselves." He heard Clyde try to laugh.

"I wish I had," Danny muttered. His voice hardly sounded like his own. His throat was dry and parched and the words seemed to stick before they were out.

"What was that?"

"Nothing."

Clyde pulled gently at him. "Come on. Can you get up? Are you all right?"

"Leave me alone. I can get up by myself." He was unsteady on his feet, and it took all his control not to fall down again, but he didn't. His head ached, and he still heard the ringing in his ears. "Water," Danny said in a voice that still didn't sound right.

It was Mr. Thompson who handed him a canteen, and Danny drank as if he hadn't had

water for days. "You okay, Danny?" Mr.
Thompson asked anxiously.

Clyde spoke before Danny had time to answer. "Sure he's okay. Ain't you, boy? No broken bones. A little fight never hurt anyone.
Come on, we better be getting back on the trail
of that bear before it gets to New Hampshire."

"I'm not going," Danny told him. "I never
wanted to. . . ."

"What do you mean? Willy's still coming, and
you gave him some workout."

"That don't matter," Danny replied, and he
wished his voice sounded more like his own.

Clyde put his arm around Danny. "Look,
boy. If you're not feeling well, we can take a
break here. I guess I handed you quite a wal-
lop. I didn't mean . . ."

Danny pulled away. "I just don't want to go
on the hunt!" he shouted in his hoarse voice.

"Hey, Danny, wait a minute. You're the
guide on this hunt. Besides, you did yourself
proud. You got nothing to run from," Clyde
said, and Danny thought he was pleading.

Danny couldn't stand hearing Clyde plead
with him. It was wrong. All mixed up. He was
tired. He wanted to get away from Clyde, from
everyone.

"Come on, Danny." It was Clyde. Danny

closed him out. The throbbing in his eye was growing worse, and every muscle in his body was screaming for him to lie down again. For a moment he was afraid his feet were going to fold under him. "I'm leaving, Clyde," he shouted suddenly, desperately.

Clyde reached out for him. "All right, boy. We'll go back together—"

"No! Leave me alone, Clyde. Just leave me alone!" Wiping the blood from his eyes, he turned to leave, but Mr. Thompson was standing there, blocking his way.

"Danny—" he began.

"Leave me alone. Everyone just leave me alone!" Danny shouted, pushing Mr. Thompson aside as he took off, racing down the mountain.

Chapter Fourteen

Beth opened the book pressing her flower necklace, and touching the wilted, drying petals,
she remembered how the bears made her feel
so happy, excited, special. She thought of the
cub rummaging through the bushes searching
for berries, and how she laughed the time it
stood up and nipped its mother playfully on
the ear. But most of all she remembered the
mother bear raging on the top of the incline, so
strong and beautiful. . . . Then she remembered the hunters with their guns—that was
frightening. She didn't want to think and re-

member anymore. "I wish I'd never even seen the bears. Go away bears! Go away and leave me alone!" she cried, slamming the book shut.

But the memory of the bears stayed with her, and she went outside to escape from her thoughts. She walked slowly through the field and went for a long gentle ride on the swing.

As she was swinging, she seemed to forget about the bears for a while, concentrating on pumping and the way the swinging made her feel. She thought about swinging so high she would fly to the top of the old oak. She thought about going into town after supper with her father and getting ice cream at Peggy Dwyer's. She tried to remember all she'd done alone on the mountain last week when the bears were her secret. The bears—always and finally her thoughts came back to the bears. So she stayed on the swing a while longer, telling their story to the old oak again. She knew the old oak understood and suffered silently with her.

At last, Beth let the swing come slowly to a stop and slid off, turning to go home. Danny was at the edge of the tall grass, staring at her.

"Get away!" she ordered. "This is my swing. I don't want you here. You're a murderer and a liar. I don't want a murderer here. This is a sacred place. My place. Murderers aren't allowed!"

Danny stood motionless, and Beth wondered if he'd understood her. She noticed the cut above his eye was much worse than the other day and his nose was swollen; but she didn't care what had happened to him. He deserved it and more.

Danny had understood her; but he didn't know what to answer. He'd come to Beth for a reason, but now he couldn't say what he'd come to say.

"Did you understand? I said this is *my* place. Now get out of here, Danny!"

"It's my place, too," he said softly, his head down. When everything else in his life was going wrong, he still had the swing. But it was her swing, too, he realized—it was something they shared; and, for the first time, that sharing seemed important.

"Danny, I can't understand you if you don't look at me," Beth said angrily.

Danny looked up. "I'm sorry . . ." he began, scarcely moving his mouth as he spoke.

"I can't understand," she said impatiently.

"I said . . ." But he couldn't get out the words "I'm sorry" again—not with her staring so angrily at him. "Nothing." He shrugged.

"Then leave me alone."

As he turned to leave, he remembered something. Looking back, he said to her, "Clyde is home. They didn't catch the bears. They didn't even see them. But they're going out again tomorrow." And then he added hopefully, "I bet they give up if they don't get them tomorrow. And I bet they don't get them!"

Beth stared blankly at him.

"Didn't you understand?"

She wanted to jump up and down, laughing and shouting, but she didn't want Danny to know how happy he'd made her. She nodded. "Now leave me alone," she said, turning away.

Danny tapped her gently. "There's something else, Beth. I'm not gonna go on the hunt tomorrow. And I didn't stay today. I left. Remember I promised you I wouldn't ever hunt the bears?"

"What do your promises mean anyway?"

Danny had no answer. He turned and ran back across the field.

As soon as he left, Beth grinned. Her heart was beating so fast, she had to take a deep breath to calm herself. *My bears are safe! They're safe!*

"They're safe, Mr. Oak!" she called as she jumped on the swing. Pushing back as far as she could, and standing on the tips of her toes, she boosted the swing into the air. Letting her head fall down and arching her back, she flew through the air, delighting in the pleasure of the swing's wide sweeping movements. Everything was right with the world again, and she laughed with the happiness bursting inside her.

Only later, as she relaxed on a more gently swaying swing, did she think about Danny. There had been something strange about the way he'd acted before. First he stared at her as if *he* were deaf. Then he talked to himself. Then he said he had nothing to say. And then he told her about the bears. Maybe that was the strangest of all. Why had he even bothered to tell her?

Maybe it's because of the bears, she decided. *They heard me after all! That's why Danny came to the swing. The bears have some power over him, and they made him come to tell me they were safe! They wanted to thank me for warning them, but they couldn't, so they sent Danny instead!*

Stopping the swing, she turned to the oak and said, "What do you think, Mr. Oak? I know it sounds silly but in a way it makes sense. The Indians could communicate with animals—so why can't I? Besides, if I found the bears every day last week, then why couldn't the hunters? There's only one answer to that, Mr. Oak. Because the bears heard me, and they went away—far, far away where the hunters will never find them. Never!"

~

"Are you sure you're all right?" Mrs. Grady asked Danny when he came home.

If you ask me that once more, he thought, *I'm going to explode.* Instead, he nodded.

"Well, why don't you sit down with us, then? We're just having some coffee," she went on.

"No, thanks," Danny mumbled.

"Come on, boy. I didn't really get a chance to tell you about the rest of the hunt. . . ." Clyde said cheerfully.

"I don't want to hear about it!" Danny cut him off, turning to leave again.

"Where you going?" his mother asked.

"Out."

"But you just came in."

"I changed my mind! Don't I have a right to do that?" he shouted, slamming the door behind him. But he didn't go far—there was no place to go. Beth was still at the swing—he could hear her laughing.

"It's the pressure," he heard his mother say as he sat down on the porch steps. "His father was like that, too. Easy going until he was pushed too far, and then he'd explode."

"I wasn't pushing him, Alice. No more than I

had to. You know something? I believe that little deaf girl was telling the truth about the bears. And that's a mighty powerful thing Danny had to defend himself against."

Danny froze. *Clyde doesn't believe me!* He felt as though a thick, cold fog was surrounding him, sucking him in, making his mouth go dry and his heart thud in his brain.

"Clyde Grady! How can you sit there and call your son a liar!" Mrs. Grady cried out.

"Because it's what I feel is true."

"Then why didn't you question him about it?"

"I couldn't. You should have seen how he turned on me this morning. Like he had a whole lifetime of hatred against me. I tell you, Alice, it scared me."

"Don't be silly. Danny's not a hateful boy. And besides, he's been much better toward you these past days. I know he was pleased you liked the new fencing."

"Well, that's what I thought. But after this morning . . ." he sighed sadly. "I never dreamed he was lying about the bear. I tell you I was shocked when Beth said what she said."

"But you don't know for certain that Danny's lying. It's hard to believe. Danny's not a liar by nature."

"I'm as certain as I can be, short of his coming out and admitting it. If you could have seen his face when Beth called him a liar. He got white as a sheet, and he didn't even defend, himself. Not really. I had to do it for him. He just stood there with his head bent over."

Mrs. Grady was silent for a few moments, and then she said, "I don't see Beth lying any more than I do Danny. It's strange. I wonder what went on between them in the first place for something like this to happen?"

Clyde sighed. "To tell you the truth, I don't think anything would have come of it if it wasn't for Willy. He sensed Danny was lying, and he was on him right away about how a little deaf girl had to save him. He out-and-out called Danny a liar and a chicken—Danny had to stand up to that. He had to answer it then or Willy would have lorded it over him forever."

"Wait a minute. I don't understand you. First you say Danny's lying and now you say he had to fight to prove he wasn't lying."

"He had to prove he wasn't afraid, Alice. Don't you see? There would have been no shame to the truth if Danny had come out with it from the very beginning. But lying like he did, and having Beth call him out in front of all those men, and on top of that, Willy—there just wasn't any choice but that he had to make his stand with Willy."

"Maybe. Maybe not . . . . Oh, I know you did what you thought best; but pushing Danny isn't the way. You should have let him and Willy work it out themselves."

"It would have been wrong for him to walk away from Willy. I'll always believe that."

"But, Clyde—Danny's not a fighter. . . ."

"A man doesn't walk away from a fight, Alice . . ."

"Oh, stop it! That's ridiculous. What do you want? For Danny to be spending his life fighting?"

"No, but there's a time to fight and a time not to fight. And this was the time to fight."

"Maybe it was the time for you to fight, but it wasn't Danny's time. You can't make him into something he's not."

"I'm not trying to. But there's certain things the boy's got to know about. That's why he needs a father."

"There are lots of things he needs a father for, Clyde; and fighting isn't one of them. Lying is. I tell you, if you're so sure Danny lied, then you got to talk to him about it."

"Short of tying him down to a chair, there's no way I can talk to him now. You should have seen him when I came home before. He was sitting on the porch, and I called to him. I was hoping we could talk. Not about anything serious, just talk and maybe ease things up. But he looked away from me and ran into the field."

"Maybe he's ashamed to face you. . . ."

"Ashamed of what? Not of his fighting. He fought like a man, and I told him so."

"Of his lie."

"But I never let on I thought he was lying."

"That doesn't change the fact of his lie and everything that's happened because of it. He lied to get out of something that he must have thought was bad, something he was troubled about. But the lie didn't help. It only made other things happen, worse than what he first feared. He's hurting, Clyde. He needs a father now."

"Maybe he does, but I'm not the father he needs. He's made that clear enough."

"But you came so far with him last week. You can't give up now."

"I'm not giving up. That's the last thing I'm doing. But I know when I'm beat. The next step's gotta come from him. I feel like he's taken all the good that was between us and thrown it in my face. I've done everything I could with him. It's time he learns to be a little accepting of me, too. It's been more than two years since we got married, and I feel farther from that boy than I did on our wedding day."

Danny shivered suddenly. He had to get away from there. As he raced across the field, he hoped Beth had gone home. He needed to be alone. To think. To make sense of it all, at least to try. *Clyde knows about the lie. He's known all along. And he didn't call me out on it. He doesn't hate me for what I did. . . . And if that's true, then I lied for nothing.*

He stared at the empty, motionless swing for a few moments, then reached out to touch it, making it zigzag back and forth. *If it's true. But maybe it isn't. Maybe he's just saying that to make himself look good with Ma. . . .* Suddenly he grabbed the ropes. "I hate you, Clyde! I always have, and I always will!" But even as he spoke the words, he knew he didn't feel that hatred inside him anymore. If he hated anyone, it was himself.

He sat down against the tree and stared intently at the rock as if the peace he sought were there; but, for the first time, being there, in his place, didn't ease the pain and confusion inside him. *How could I have been so wrong? Why didn't I tell the truth? Maybe it wasn't so terrible. . . .*

If only he hadn't lied. If only he could go

back to before the lie when Clyde was pleased with his work on the fencing. Then he could clean up the barn, get a horse, paint the store, and—work things out with Clyde. He never realized until now how much he wanted to please Clyde. Clutching his fists and banging them on the ground, he shouted, "But I didn't mean to lie. I didn't mean to. I didn't . . ." He lay down on the ground, his arms stretched across the rock, his head pressed against it. Tears welled up inside him, and he cried.

Chapter Fifteen

Danny left the house early the next morning to feed the hogs, before either Clyde or his mother was awake. He didn't want to be around when Clyde set off for the hunt. It was only seven-thirty when he finished the chores— a whole day ahead of him and nothing to do. As he passed by the sties again and rubbed his hands against the newly painted fencing, he thought of checking out the barn. Maybe he could get started cleaning it out today. But as he stood in front of the barn, staring at the unhinged door, he began to change his mind.

Maybe he didn't really feel like spending his day in the musty old barn. Maybe Clyde wouldn't want him to anymore. . . .

He looked at his watch. Hank was probably getting up just about now. He had to be at work by eight-thirty, and it took almost a half-hour for him to bike to the mall. Danny decided to call Hank and see if he could use the guitar today. That was better than cleaning out the barn anyway.

The door to the store was locked so Danny climbed in through a back window of the smokehouse. Hank answered the phone.

"Hank! This is Danny."

"Danny? What's up? Anything wrong?"

"No. I just wanted to get you before you left. I was thinking of coming over and practicing."

"Now? It's kind of early."

"No. Later, but I thought I'd call. . . ."

"Okay. Hold on a minute—" Danny could hear Hank calling to his mother. He could hear Mrs. Thompson's voice but he couldn't make out what she was saying. "Yeah, it's fine," Hank finally answered. "Nobody's gonna be here, but there's always a key under the big geranium pot out back."

"You sure it's okay?"

"Sure. You can have the whole place to make as much noise as you want!" He laughed.

Paused. And began again. "Hey, Danny—Dad told me about Willy and Clyde yesterday."

Danny cut him off with a careless laugh. "That's the way it goes. Look, I gotta go." He didn't want to talk to Hank about yesterday. He didn't want to know if Hank and his father thought he was lying, too. He wished he'd never called. "I'm at the store, and I got some things I promised Ma I'd do."

He was lowering the phone from his ear when he heard Hank say, "It sounded pretty rough. I wish I'd been there. You and me, we could have handed it to that punk, Willy! Huh?"

Danny breathed deeply, and for a moment he couldn't answer. He should have known Hank would stick up for him. "Yeah, I sure could have used some help."

"Clyde giving you a rough time?"

"Not so bad. I mean . . . I don't know what I mean. It's crazy, Hank. Really crazy . . ." He choked up and couldn't go on.

"Man, I wish I didn't have this crummy job to go to. We could just hang around for a while—play the guitar."

All Danny could do was nod.

"Ma said you've only been over practicing a few times," Hank said.

Danny swallowed. "Well, I was fixing the

sties for Clyde. He paid me. But that's over now. It's gonna be a lousy summer. I can tell."

"I got Fridays and Sundays off. Why don't you come over Friday, and I'll give you some more lessons. Or maybe you could give me some!"

"Sounds okay by me. I got no plans—that's for sure!"

"Okay. See you then. Come over early."

"Hey, I was thinking," Danny suggested, "I could meet you up at Route 9 and ride with you to work this morning."

"I thought you had things to do for your mother."

"I got time. You won't be here for a while."

"Let's see. I probably get near the smoke-house about eight-fifteen."

"I'll be waiting."

"Okay, Danny. See you then."

Danny held on to the phone for a moment, squeezing it tightly. *I should have called Hank last night,* he thought; and he felt himself smiling.

~

Beth watched the deer from her bedroom window as they circled through the field on their path, stopping now and then, flicking their ears, moving on so naturally . . . as if nothing terrible could be happening. Maybe they, too, knew the bears had escaped. . . .

"Let's go fishing today," she said to her father at breakfast.

"Well, I'm glad to see you in better spirits. I think fishing sounds like a great idea."

"When you come back, we can pack a picnic and go down to the lake for a swim," her mother suggested.

The fishing was terrific—better than Beth had ever known it. She caught three big bass, and her father caught four.

"If we keep going, we'll have to open a fish market," he teased.

Beth laughed; but she had her own ideas about the fishing. *The fish are a gift from the bears,* she thought. *Another good omen. It is just like the Indians said.*

"Do you think human beings and animals can talk to each other?" she asked her father. "I don't mean really talk like people—but I think there's something about nature. I mean, if a person loves nature and animals, the animals know it. Like dogs can tell when a person is afraid. Maybe a person who loves nature becomes a part of nature—like the animals."

"What made you think of that?" her father asked.

"I don't know. Maybe it's because we were studying the Indians in school. There were some tribes who even believed that animals like the bear were sacred. They said the bear was their brother. And that's what I think, too. That's why I wasn't even scared when the bear chased Danny and me. At first I was, but later, when I was safe in the tree—I really wasn't scared. I looked at the bear. She was so big and strong and beautiful, Daddy!"

"Did she make any sound? Could you hear it?"

Beth nodded. "She roared. And I did hear it! That was scary—but just a little." She thought for a moment and then giggled. "You know what it reminded me of?"

Mr. Hampton shook his head.

"The subway!"

"The subway?" He raised his eyebrows dubiously and laughed.

"It did!"

"Okay, okay! I believe you. After all, you were there. I wasn't! But imagine—the Lexington Avenue subway on Mt. Ash!"

Beth laughed. "Well, maybe it wasn't so loud as the subway, but it was loud—and anyway, you didn't answer my question."

He thought for a moment and asked, "About animals and people talking?"

"Not talking—talking like people do. I think maybe there are special times when people and

animals can understand each other. Not all the
time. Not when you're just walking through the
woods and stuff like that. But sometimes. Like
. . . like when they're in trouble."

"Well, I don't know about that, but I'd say we
had something special with us today—catching
all these fish. I can't ever remember having
such a good day fishing. Can you?"

"Nope." Beth grinned and nodded. "Maybe
the bears are thanking us," she added.

"What was that?"

"Oh, nothing . . ."

~

"I think we should have fish for lunch here
and then go to the lake," Mrs. Hampton said
when she saw their catch.

"Just what I hoped you'd say," Mr. Hampton
quickly agreed. But after lunch he was too full
to go swimming. "I'm too stuffed to move,
much less swim," he told Beth. "Besides, I'd
probably sink. Do you mind if we go later?"

Beth shook her head.

"Good, then I think I'll take a nap."

"That sounds like a wonderful idea," her
mother agreed. "The heat is getting to me.
What are you going to do, Beth?"

"I don't know. Maybe I'll go into town and
get an ice cream."

"An ice cream!" her father cried. "How can you even think of it?"

Beth giggled. "Maybe I'll get a hot fudge sundae—if you give me the money."

Her father moaned. "I'll give you anything you want if you don't mention food again!"

～

Danny was sitting in Peggy Dwyer's when Beth came in, figuring out some numbers on a napkin as he drank his soda. *$1.80 an hour . . . at six hours a night, that's $10.80 . . . $75.60 a week . . . $151.20 in two weeks . . .* With the twenty dollars from Clyde and a little bit more he had saved, he and Hank could go into Montpelier and get a second-hand guitar. . . . Of course, it wasn't certain he'd get the job. He told the man he was fifteen, almost sixteen. That was Hank's idea. Danny wasn't so sure, but Hank must have been right because the man took his name and phone number and told him he'd call in a few days. Hank applied for a job, too. It was only for two weeks, working at the traveling amusement park going up at the parking lot at the mall. Danny had spent the morning watching them put up the rides. Then at lunch, he and Hank had applied for the jobs.

Beth sat as far away from Danny as possible.

"Well, Beth, what'll it be today?" Peggy asked.

"Hot fudge sundae with peppermint-stick ice cream!"

Danny looked up at the sound of Beth's voice, but quickly turned away.

"Maybe you can tell me what happened with that bear, Beth?" Peggy asked. "I tried to get a first-hand description from Danny, but he's too busy scribbling on that napkin to talk."

What did she have to come in here for now? Danny thought as he hurriedly put a quarter on the counter, stuffed the napkin with his figuring in his pocket, and started for the door.

"Danny and I have different stories," Beth said bitterly. And turning to Danny, she demanded, "Don't we?"

Before Danny could answer, the door was opened, and Mrs. Willard burst in, waving her hands excitedly and talking too fast for Beth to understand. Then she hurried back outside again.

"What is it?" Beth asked Peggy.

Peggy's answer was lost to Beth as Peggy hurried toward the door.

"Danny!" Beth shouted. "What's happening?"

Danny turned to look at Beth. He opened his

171

mouth to speak, then shook his head and ran out after Peggy. Beth followed, and when she got outside, she saw a crowd forming at the other end of Main Street. *Maybe it's the bears!* she thought frantically and began running. *But it can't be. My bears are safe. I know it!* she tried to assure herself as she ran faster and faster. When she reached the crowd, she stopped suddenly, almost afraid of what was ahead of her.

Danny had stopped before he even reached the crowd. From where he was he could already see enough to know he wanted to be no closer—heading toward town were the hunters. Willy, Brian, and Willy's father were in the lead, with Willy and Brian carrying guns across their shoulders like soldiers on review. Behind them were Albert Townley and Red, bent over and sweating under the weight of their heavy load: hanging upside down from the pole they carried between them was the mother bear. She was tied by her legs, and she hung in a dead heap, her head doubling over against her back as her body dragged and pulled against the road. Behind Red came Clyde and Mr. Willard. They were carrying a pole between them, too: the bear cub hung from it—its mouth open, its eyes wide.

A cheer went through the crowd, and Danny

watched Willy and Brian as they jumped up and down, raising their guns triumphantly into the air. His eyes skipped from hunter to hunter until he came to Clyde, who was smiling along with the others, his face red and dripping with perspiration. As his eyes rested on Clyde's, he felt suddenly certain that Clyde was grinning at him. He didn't want Clyde or anyone from the hunting party to see him, so he ran to the cover of some nearby trees.

Beth pushed her way to the front of the crowd as the cheering swelled to a roar around her. For a moment she couldn't breath or move. Then her hands shot up, covering her ears, and she was screaming. "My bears! My bears!" But in all the noise and confusion, nobody heard her or noticed the terror in her face.

The crowd opened up as the hunters drew near and then closed around them, marching along beside them as they made their way down Main Street toward the statue of the Revolutionary War hero. Pushed and shoved along by the onlookers, Beth tripped and scraped her knee, but she hardly felt it—her eyes remained riveted on the mother bear's face. She gasped in horror as Mr. Townley and Red dropped the beautiful mother bear in a heap in front of the statue. Tears of anger and unhappiness burned her eyes as she watched Clyde and Mr. Willard lift the pole with the cub high into the air, and drop it next to its mother.

A numb dulling pain ran up and down her body, and she felt frozen until she saw something that made her anger explode: Willy and Brian and some older kids, poking the cub with sticks. In an instant she was on top of Willy, hitting him and punching him. "Leave my bears alone! Leave them alone!"

Brian yanked her off, throwing her to the ground; but Beth was up again, ready to attack. "If you touch my bears again—I'll kill you!" she shouted, but nobody could understand her. Looking from Willy to the crowd of people surrounding them, she cried out, "Go away! Leave my bears alone!"

People noticed Beth now, but nobody answered, nobody moved; they stared back at her with helpless, anxious expressions on their faces. Danny watched Beth, too, from his hiding place. Her anger was so terrible and painful it made him shudder. He wanted to help her, but his body refused to move from the safety of the tree. He couldn't let Willy see him now.

It was Willy who spoke out first. "Can't understand you, dummy. Can you repeat it? Please?" he tormented her, imitating her sounds.

She went for him again; but somebody grabbed her, holding her back. It was Mr. Clarke.

"Let me go!" Beth demanded, struggling to get free, but Mr. Clarke held her tightly, trying to calm her down. He shooed the boys away and took Beth outside the crowd where Mrs. Clarke was standing with Jamie, Carrie, and Timothy, in a stroller. When she saw Mrs. Clarke, she began to cry.

Danny felt helpless and miserable as he watched Beth wrap her arms around Mrs. Clarke, and heard her broken, gasping sobs. *I'm worse than Willy and Brian—it's all my fault. Everything.* He had to get away. He had to be alone. Away from all the noise. Away from Clyde and the hunters. Away from Willy and Brian. Away from the bears. And away from Beth. He ran up through the woods to escape to the swing.

~

"Come on, Beth. Come and sit down on the bench," Mrs. Clarke said, but she couldn't get Beth to look at her; and so she stroked her hair and held her until her crying stopped.

"The bears," Beth sobbed. "The bears—they're dead."

Mrs. Clarke pulled away from Beth, and as Beth looked up at her, she said, "Let me take you home?"

Beth shook her head. She didn't want to go home. She wanted to go to the swing.

Chapter Sixteen

Danny panicked at the sound of feet running
on the deer trail. *It's Beth,* he thought, jumping
off the swing. *I should have known she'd come here.*
And he began to run. She needed the swing
more than he did now.

The swing was still jerking in wide, awkward
movements when Beth reached it, but she
didn't notice. Breathless, she ran to the old oak
and fell against it. Not having the strength to
move, she leaned against the tree, spreading
out her arms, hugging it, rubbing her face
against the bark. Her head was pounding and

her heart was beating furiously. She couldn't let go of the tree. She felt she would die if she did, so she hugged it and cried. It was awful, terrible—everything in the whole world—and she was so alone.

"Why?" she begged to the old oak. "Why did they kill my bears?"

Lying down on the soft grass under the oak, she pressed her burning face against the cool earth. Every time she thought she could stop crying, she'd think of the bears and her body trembled, her throat and eyes burned and she cried harder. She wasn't crying out of anger anymore or even hatred, but from an overwhelming loneliness. Everything seemed lost to her now.

How could I think I was so special? How could I think the bears were sending me messages—me, deaf and dumb. Dumb. Dumb. Stupid! Stupid! Stupid! I was wrong. People are people, and bears are bears. Bears can't think. They can't talk. And if they could, they wouldn't have thought about me! She remembered thinking the fish were a gift from the bears. It seemed a cruel joke now.

Slowly she stood up and walked over to the swing, sat down, and began pushing at the ground with her feet. Slowly, so slowly, she made the swing sway back and forth. As she kicked the ground under her foot, little specks of dirt flew into the hot heavy air. She began swinging higher and higher, faster and faster; and as she did, she screamed and cried out loud, all the most terrible, awful noises she could make. She screamed and cried until her throat hurt and her head felt as though it might explode. When she came to a stop and got off the swing, her mother and father were standing there.

"Is it the bears?" her mother asked.

Beth nodded.

"I'm sorry, Beth. So sorry," her mother said and moved toward her.

"It doesn't matter anymore," she told her mother angrily. She watched her mother pull away, hurt. This time Beth didn't care if she hurt her mother's feelings. She wanted to hurt something back, she hurt so much herself. She wanted the whole world to hurt with her. "They're dead," she cried accusingly.

Her father said, "Let's go home," and tried to take Beth's hand.

"No! I don't want to go home! I want to stay here!"

"You'll feel better at home. It's so hot here. Come on, you're trembling."

Beth wanted to say no again. She wanted her parents to leave, but she didn't have the strength to argue anymore. She went to her room as soon as they reached the cottage and lay down on her bed. It was even hotter inside than it had been outside. The heat seemed to be closing in on her, suffocating her.

Maybe I'll die from the heat. And that's okay. It's okay with me.

But soon the room was so stifling that she got up and took an icy shower. Then she went to her father.

"What will they do with the bears now that they've killed them?" she asked.

Her father shook his head. "I don't know."

"Why? Why did they do such a terrible thing?"

Again her father shook his head.

"They tied the bears to poles and dragged them into town." Her voice was hoarse from crying, and her father could barely make out her words.

"I'm sorry, Beth."

It wasn't enough for Beth. Her father didn't feel as she did, so he couldn't understand her pain. Beth nodded sadly and said, "It's hot in my room."

"Why don't you lie down in the living room? I'll set up the fan."

The fan didn't help much, and the afternoon dragged on and on. She was too exhausted to do anything, and she was too nervous to lie around and do nothing. She tried to sleep, but every time she closed her eyes, she saw the face of the dead bear cub. *It was so beautiful—why did it have to die? Why?* There had to be a reason. The only one she could come up with was Danny. He broke the pact. He lied. And that's why her bears were dead. She'd told the truth, but nobody listened to her. Nobody understood. Nobody cared. Nobody wanted to save the bears. They only wanted to blame them, hunt them, and kill them—for nothing, because the bears did nothing. The blame belonged to Danny. All of it. And that mattered. Somehow it had to matter—*because I know it does! It matters to me!*

Beth hardly ate dinner even though her father grilled hot dogs and her mother bought marshmallows.

"Want to go for a walk?" her father asked later.

Beth shook her head. "I just want to be alone."

"I know it hurts now. But it will pass. You'll never forget the bears, but the pain will pass."

"I know," she muttered, but she didn't believe him.

~

Danny was lying on the bed when his mother came in. "Can I talk to you?" she asked.

"If you want. But I got nothing to talk about."

"You didn't eat your supper. And you've been up here all by yourself all afternoon. I know something is bothering you."

"No. I'm just not hungry."

She sat down on the bed next to him and tried to brush the hair out of his eyes. Danny pushed her hand away.

"What's the matter?" she asked tenderly.

"Nothing, Ma. I just want to be alone. Why do you always make such a big deal when I want to be alone?"

"Danny, I know when something's bothering you."

"Nothing's bothering me!"

"You sure?"

"Yeah!"

"All right then," she sighed as she got up to leave.

When she was almost to the door, Danny cried out, "I'll tell you what's bothering me! I think it was disgusting the way Clyde brought the bears into town!"

Mrs. Grady turned around, surprised. "But why? The men meant no harm. They were just proud."

"What's to be proud of? It was disgusting seeing the bears dead like that. But that wouldn't bother Clyde. He's used to disgusting things!"

"Danny, don't—don't talk like that."

"Why not? I'll talk any way I want about him. I don't care about him. Why should I? Everything that's rotten and stinking is because of him!"

Mrs. Grady sat down next to Danny again; but when she reached for his hand, he pulled away. "That's not true, Danny. You're angry and upset, and you're blaming it on Clyde."

"I'm not listening to you, Ma!" he shouted, covering his ears with his hands. "All you do is stick up for him, like you always do."

"That's not true."

"You do! You're sticking up for him now just like you did when he made me slaughter that cow."

Pulling his hands away from his ears, she said, "Now you listen to me, Danny. I wasn't siding with him then. I didn't side with either of you. Clyde needed help, and you owed it to him to try. That's all I asked from you, that you try. And you did. What happened later didn't matter."

"That's why you went along with him when he said I had to feed the hogs!"

"There's nothing wrong with you helping around the smokehouse. And look at the fine job you did on the sties. That made you proud. I know it did."

Danny didn't want to be reminded of that. He slammed his fists down on the bed and shouted, "Why'd you marry him, Ma? We would have been all right without him!"

For a moment the pain and anger in Danny's voice echoed about them so loudly that his mother couldn't answer. "Danny," she began softly, and her voice quivered, "what do you think it would have been like, just you and me alone?"

"It would have been fine. It would have been perfect. It's what Dad would have wanted!"

"It isn't. Andy would have wanted you to grow up with a regular family."

"No. He would have wanted just you and me to stay together. Just you and me, Ma. Then nothing would have changed."

"Danny, don't you see—everything changed when he died."

"No! Everything changed when you married Clyde! You promised you'd always love me best. You told me that, Ma. But you don't. Not anymore!"

He'd said it. He'd finally said it. But it didn't make him feel any better. He felt worse.

"Oh, Danny," she cried, putting her arms around him; and this time he didn't pull away. He held on to her tightly as he did the night his father died, feeling warmed by her touch and comforted by the soft sadness in her voice.

Wiping the tears from his face, she said, "It's not so simple as you're trying to make it. It's not just a matter of who loves who best. There's not a person or thing in this world I love better than you. You're a part of your father. Sometimes I look at you and I see Andy, and I just want to burst into tears. I can even hear him in your voice lately. The older you get, the more like him you're growing, and I think how much he would have wanted to see you grow. But it wasn't meant to be, Danny. No matter how much we may want him here with us. . . ." She sighed deeply and tears began to streak her cheeks. "It'll never be again. But do you think I've forgotten him? Do you think my heart doesn't break sometimes for wanting him. There's not another man I could love like I loved your father. But Clyde's a good man. I wouldn't have married him if he wasn't. He's got a lot of feelings for you. He loves you, Danny. But you've got him as confused and unhappy as you've got yourself. Don't you see? Fighting Clyde isn't going to bring Andy back. That doesn't mean you stop thinking about

Andy and loving him—but you gotta stop putting Clyde up against him, thinking how different it would be if Andy was here instead."

"No, I can't! I can't ever stop thinking that. There wouldn't be any slaughtering with Dad. And he wouldn't have called the hunt. He wouldn't have made me lie!"

"You mean about Beth and the bears?" Mrs. Grady asked cautiously.

"Yes! I lied! It was just like Beth said it was. If it wasn't for her, the bear would have killed me!"

"But Clyde didn't make you lie."

"Yes, he did!"

"How can that be?"

"He did, that's all."

"That's no explanation."

"Because . . . because . . . I had to lie because if Clyde knew Beth had saved me, he would have hated me! He'd think I was chicken—just like Willy and Brian think . . ."

"Danny, Clyde knew you were lying when you had that run-in with Beth and her father on the mountain. But he didn't hate you for it. Instead he defended you in front of all those people. Don't you see? There was no shame to being afraid of the bears. Maybe in Willy's eyes, but Willy doesn't count. He'd have been just as scared as you, I guarantee it. It was the lying that was wrong."

"Then why did he defend me?" Danny cried, feeling more confused than ever.

"Because he loves you, Danny. And he knew you needed him then, no matter what you'd done."

"I can't believe that, Ma. He did it 'cause he didn't want to look bad!"

"That's not true, Danny. You talk like Clyde is your enemy. Like he's out to get you. But if you'd just give him a chance, you'd find he's not against you, even if he doesn't always agree with you. There's no harm in disagreeing or having an argument. It's going to happen. It would have happened with Andy. But if there are some good feelings between you, then there's a chance of working out the problems."

"But he's always pushing me, Ma, making me do things I don't want to do. He never thinks about me and what I want!"

"I don't think he really knows what you want," she said sadly. "I don't think he really knows you, and that's as much a part of the problem as anything. But the fact is, you've never given him a chance to know you. You've always been so busy fighting him. See, Danny, you have to be a little understanding of Clyde, too. It's not easy starting to be a father of a half-grown boy at the age of forty-five. He's set in his ways. And he's stubborn some and even a little pigheaded at times. . . ."

"Maybe that's why he and Seymour get along so well!"

Mrs. Grady laughed. "Sometimes I see more than a passing resemblance between you and Seymour, too!"

Danny shrugged but couldn't help smiling a little.

"Don't you see, Danny? There has to be some giving in from both sides. Clyde's willing. I know he is. He's sitting downstairs right now, just sick over this whole thing. All he needs to know is that you're willing to try again."

"You make it sound so simple, Ma!" he protested. "I mess up everything."

"Now don't you go feeling sorry for yourself, Danny Grady, because you'll get no sympathy from me. Nothing's been messed up so bad it can't be straightened out. But if you want to feel sorry for someone, let it be Beth. It seems to me she's suffered more than anyone because of all this. Clyde said she was just miserable in town today when she saw the bears."

"Don't you think I know that?"

"Well . . ." she said hesitantly, "I wasn't sure."

"I tried to tell her I was sorry. But she won't listen to me. She just gets angry."

"Can you blame her?"

"But what can I do? I can't bring back the bears."

"No, you can't do that. I don't know, maybe there's nothing you can do."

"Ma, I'm sorry! I really am. I didn't mean to lie. I didn't want to hurt Beth."

"I know that, Danny, but that doesn't erase all the problems . . . Maybe if things change between you and Clyde, it'll be worth it."

"Not for Beth."

"No, not for Beth . . ."

Danny sat glumly on the bed. He shoved a magazine lying near him onto the floor.

"Come on, Danny. It's not so bleak. I promise." She bent over to kiss him. "You'll see. Things will work out."

"I want them to, Ma. I do!" he burst out.

She smiled. "Well, that's half the battle, Danny. Maybe more than half . . . Now why don't you come down and eat?"

He sighed, then nodded. "Yeah, I guess I am hungry."

"All right then—I'll go heat up the stew."

Danny started down a little while later, but he stopped near the top of the stairs. Clyde and his mother were in the hall. He could hear them talking. He didn't want to interrupt them, so went back to his room. *I'll go down when the stew's ready,* he told himself.

He sat on his bed, looking out the window. There were no stars and the moon was streaked with misty clouds. *It's gonna rain tomorrow,* he thought. *I hope it holds off till I feed the hogs. Then maybe I'll start on the barn. . . . Not much else to do on a rainy day.*

Suddenly something thudded against the side of the house near his window; then a voice called, "Danny! Oh, Danny boy!" It was Willy.

"What do you want?" he demanded.

"We want you to come down, Danny boy. We got a surprise for you!" Willy answered.

"Kinda like a present," Brian added.

"Yeah, a present!" Willy laughed.

"Come on, please!" Brian pleaded mockingly. "There's someone out here just dying to go for a swing, Danny!"

"Get lost!" Danny shouted back.

"Ain't you coming?" Willy taunted. "It's a friend of yours!"

Danny slammed shut the window; but he could still hear Willy and Brian laughing, calling for him. He decided not to answer—he wasn't going to give them the satisfaction. Still, he worried. Maybe they'd done something to the swing. Once, when he and Willy had been really close, he'd told Willy a little about the swing. Not much, but enough for Willy to know the swing was important.

He thought of going to check out the swing, but he couldn't tell whether or not Willy and Brian were still around. He didn't want to run into them now, in the dark. *I'll go over in the morning, before I go to the smokehouse,* he decided. *And if they did anything, I'll get them back. I'll make Willy think what I did to him yesterday was just fun and games.*

Chapter Seventeen

Beth woke early the next morning, aching all over; her eyes were swollen from crying, and her throat hurt from screaming. It was hot and muggy. Hardly a breeze blew. The sky was dull and overcast; clouds hid the top of the mountain. It was going to be a rainy day.

She crept downstairs and poured herself some orange juice; but it burned her throat, and she didn't finish it. After sitting on the porch for a few minutes, she headed for the field and her swing. The tall grass, wet from the dew, clung to her clothes and body in damp splotches, making her itch. She pulled at the grass as she walked, crumpling and ripping it. A bee flew around her head and landed on her hair. She brushed it away with a lazy sweep of her arm. It was a sad, lonely day. Cloudy. Unhappy. The world was crying for the bears.

When she got to the edge of the tall grass, she looked, as she always did, over toward the swing. What she saw made her shiver violently. She stood perfectly still, frozen to the ground, unable to believe what she saw. It was impossible. She began running toward the swing, running as fast as she'd ever run before.

Tied to the ropes of the swing were the big, furry hands of the dead bear cub. It sat on the almost imperceptibly moving swing, its head hanging down, its chin touching its chest, its eyes still holding their tale of ugliness, terror and beauty. For the first time Beth noticed a dried trail of blood that had trickled from a bullet hole in the side of its head. The blood was black and matted now against the dark brown, curly fur.

Beth could not move. She could not take her eyes off the dead bear cub and the swing. The cub's legs dangled lifelessly to the ground. *The bear can't make the swing fly,* she cried inside. *Nothing will ever make the swing fly again.*

∿

Beth didn't know how long she stood there. Aware of nothing except the dead cub, she didn't even see Danny sitting nearby, leaning against the rock near the old oak. He saw Beth, but he sat motionless, staring at a little wooden box he held in his hands. Every so often he turned a key in its side, and as he did, music gently floated from the box.

It was a while before Beth sensed she wasn't alone. When she saw Danny, she gasped in horror. Danny looked up, but didn't speak. Beth let out a terrible shriek and lunged at him, pounding him with her fists about his head and shoulders. Danny didn't try to defend himself, but tucked his head down between his knees, grasping the music box tightly, not moving as Beth hit him with all her strength, beating him until she had no more strength left. Then she collapsed on the ground beside him.

"I hate you, Danny Grady," she groaned, her face buried in the grass. "I hate you. I wish I could kill you."

As her body slowly relaxed, Beth sat up. Danny was still sitting with his head between his knees, grasping the little wooden box. She watched him, waiting for him to do something, to say something; but he didn't move. She shook him violently. He looked up at her; and without saying a word, he handed her the music box. She didn't know what it was—she had never seen a music box before.

The curious box was old and worn, with a child's drawings painted on it. The pictures were faded but still easy to make out. A tree and a swing, green grass, a blue sky, and a yellow smiling sun were painted on the top. On the sides of the box were different colored flowers and butterflies. Beth looked for a way to open the box but it wouldn't open. She turned it over and saw holes on the bottom, covered with wire mesh. Painted in black ink were the words, "This belongs to Andrew Peter Haines."

"What is it?" Beth finally asked.

Danny took the box from her and wound it up. "It's a music box."

Beth rubbed her fingers over the childish writing on the back. "Who is Andrew Peter Haines?"

"My real father. My grandfather made this for him when he was six. My father painted it. He gave it to me."

"Is this a picture of the swing? The swing here?"

Danny nodded. "It was my father's swing.

His father put it up for him. My family used to own all the land here, where your house is and everything. It was a big farm then, but it was broken up and sold a long time ago. Now the swing belongs to a man named McIntyre. He lives in Rutland. All the land between your house and mine belongs to him. I wrote him a letter last year and asked him what he was going to do with the land. He wrote back and said he had no plans. Someday, when I grow up, I'm going to buy back all the land. Then the swing will be mine again."

The thought of the swing ever belonging to Danny made Beth furious. "No! The swing is mine! I don't care who owns the land, the swing is mine!" she shouted and pushed the music box back into Danny's hands. "It couldn't belong to someone who would tie a dead bear to it."

"What?"

"I said you tied the bear to the swing. The swing can never be yours."

"I didn't, Beth! I swear! I would never do anything like that to the swing."

"You think I believe you?"

Danny clenched his fingers around the music box. "I swear I didn't tie the bear to the swing. You have to believe me. It was here when I came this morning."

"You're such a liar. Why should I believe you?"

Danny turned the key in the music box, and as the music played, he said slowly, "I'm sorry the bears are dead, Beth. I know it's my fault. But I didn't mean to break our pact. You gotta believe me. I'm not lying now. This is my place here as much as it's yours. I couldn't lie here. I swear on the swing and this music box that I didn't tie the bear to the swing."

"Who did then?" she demanded harshly.

Danny thought for a moment and said, "Willy and Brian."

"How do you know?"

He shrugged. "I just know, that's all."

"Why should I believe you? Besides, Willy and Brian are your friends."

"Not anymore." He knelt down and picked up a plastic bag lying on the rock. He wrapped up the music box inside the bag and pulled back the rock. Underneath it was a big hole. Inside the hole was another bag. Looking at Beth, Danny went on: "This is where I keep the music box. It belongs with the swing and the rock." He thought about Pterodactyl, and was about to tell Beth about the magic of the rock, but changed his mind. Pterodactyl belonged to Danny and his father. He didn't want to share it with anyone else, so he said, "I keep things from my real father here. Do you want to see them?"

"Why are you showing them to me?" she asked hesitantly.

Her question surprised Danny and he answered the only way he could. "Because—they belong to the swing."

And Beth understood. "Yes," she nodded.

Danny handed her the bag. Inside was a child's wooden toy: a clown carved out of wood that flapped its hands and feet up and down when she pulled the string dangling from its body; a slingshot made from a branch; a rubber ball; and two photographs—one of Danny when he was small, sitting on the swing, the other of Danny and his father sitting on the swing together, Danny on his shoulders.

Beth reached into the bag for the last toy, a long wooden stick with holes in it. She shivered with excitement as she rubbed her fingers along the smooth wood, and anxiously asked, "Did your father make this flute?"

Danny nodded. "He made one for you, too."

"You remember?"

"I remember everything from that summer. It was the summer before he died. Do you still have it?"

Beth shook her head. "It got lost, but I wish

it hadn't. Your father must have been very nice to make a flute for a deaf kid." And she looked self-consciously away.

Yeah, he was nice, Danny said to himself, and he remembered how dumb he'd thought it was when his father made the flute for someone who couldn't hear. He remembered the terrible noises Beth had made as she blew on the flute, her face puffing out like a red balloon. He remembered his father getting mad at him for laughing. . . . He remembered how much his father liked Beth.

Danny tapped her, and when she looked at him he said, "This is just the same as the one he made for you. You can have it, if you want."

"But it's yours. It's from your father."

Danny thought for a moment. "Would you want to play it still? If it was yours, I mean . . ."

"I don't remember how."

"But you could learn again. It's real easy. See!" And he blew on it, showing her how to cover up the holes with her fingers.

"Blow on it again, as loud as you can," Beth asked. And she concentrated very hard until she thought she heard it. She smiled. "I think I heard that."

"No kidding?"

She nodded. "I can hear lots of sounds with my hearing aid. I think I heard your gun go off that day, and I know I heard the bear roaring."

"Beth, I want you to keep the flute," he said urgently, then casually added, "Besides, I never play it anymore. And what good is a flute if you don't play it?"

Beth took the flute from Danny. "Thanks, Danny. Thanks a lot. And I won't lose this one. I promise."

Danny felt suddenly embarrassed, and he bent down to put the clown, the slingshot, pictures and all the other things belonging with the swing back in the hole next to the music box. After he covered them with the rock, he looked back at Beth. "Nobody else knows about this place," he told her.

"I won't tell anyone."

"I know."

"Danny, I believe you now. I know you wouldn't tie the bear to the swing."

Murmuring a "thank you" that Beth couldn't see, he turned to the dead cub and untied the ropes. The swing flew back as the bear slid down, landing on the ground underneath.

"I thought I'd bury it near here," Danny told Beth. "The bear's kind of heavy. I can't move it far."

"We can bury it underneath the oak tree."

"You want to help?"

"Of course! He was my bear. . . ."

Danny didn't answer, and Beth went on, "I'll go home and get my shovel. But we only have one."

"That's okay. We have one, too. You get yours, and I'll get mine."

"Okay," Beth said and started to leave.

Danny pulled her back. "I wish it hadn't happened, Beth. I'd give anything to take it back."

Beth shivered suddenly and nodded her head. "I'll be right back," was all she said.

~

It began to rain lightly as Beth made her way through the tall grass. She put the flute underneath her shirt. The smooth, finely sanded surface felt soft and silky against her skin, and she hugged herself, pressing the flute tightly against her. *I will learn to play the flute again,* she decided. *Daddy can teach me. And when I learn, I'll go up on the mountain again and play a song for the bears.*

As she thought about it, she was filled with a strange mixture of happiness and sadness. *I wonder if they could hear me now?* And she took out the flute, blowing on it as hard as she could, moving her fingers up and down over the holes as she had seen Danny do. The sharp, loud sounds vibrated in her head, and she imagined her music was beautiful enough for the bears. Again and again she blew and each time a little more of her sadness drifted from her.

~

Her parents were sitting on the porch having coffee.

"You're up early—what's that?" her father asked.

"A flute. Danny just gave it to me. It's like the one his father made for me when I was little. Listen!" she exclaimed, blowing on it until her cheeks puffed out and her face was red.

"What's so funny?" she demanded when she opened her eyes.

"Nothing. Really, sweetheart," her father insisted. "It's just so good to see you happy again."

"Didn't it sound right?"

"It sounded perfect. Wonderful," her mother promised. "We heard you from the field."

"It sounded awful." Beth frowned. "And I imagined it was beautiful."

"Well, that's all that really counts."

"Oh, Daddy, it's not. You have to teach me the way Danny's father did. I want to learn how to blow on it right. I have to make it sound like something truly beautiful."

"I'll try," he promised. "But why did Danny give it to you? I thought you and he were arch enemies."

"Because of the swing . . ." she began, but she knew that wasn't right. It was because of the bears: he had understood about the bears, he had understood her pain—he was the only one who had. And that was strange—so strange—too strange to tell her parents.

"I can't explain now," she said abruptly. "I have to go. Danny's waiting for me at the swing. I just came back for the shovel."

"What for?" her mother asked.

Beth didn't want to tell her parents about the bear. They would certainly make a big deal about it, and her father might want to help. She didn't want his help. She wanted to bury the bear alone, with Danny.

"It's just something," she said impatiently. "I can't tell you now."

"It sounds pretty mysterious," her father teased.

"In a way it is. But I'll tell you later. I promise."

"All right," her mother said. "But get your raincoat. It might start to rain harder."

Beth nodded and went inside. But first she went to her room and put the flute next to the books pressing her flower necklace; then she got her raincoat and hurried back out. "Where's the shovel?" she asked.

"In the garage," her father answered.

As she started down the steps, she thought of something that made her turn back.

"What's the matter?" her father asked.

"I have to ask you something," she began nervously. "And I just want you to think about it. I mean, don't say no right away. Promise!"

"We can't promise . . ." her mother began.

"Oh, please. Just promise you won't say no right away."

Mr. Hampton looked at his wife and then nodded at Beth. "All right. No 'no' right away. What is it?"

"Well, I was thinking . . ." Shutting her eyes, she blurted out, "Since the bears aren't there anymore—can I go on the mountain again alone?" She was afraid to move until, after what seemed an eternity, her father tapped her.

Slowly she opened her eyes, her heart pounding. . . . Her father was smiling! So was her mother. "I don't see why not!" her father was saying.

"Oh, thank you!" she cried, hugging them both. "Thank you!" she shouted as she jumped down the porch steps and headed for the garage.

~

Danny still wasn't there when Beth got back to the swing. After a few minutes she began to worry. Maybe he wasn't coming. . . .

She was thinking of going to look for him when she saw him running across the field with his shovel.

"What took you so long?"

"I couldn't find the shovel," he said breathlessly. "At first Clyde thought he left it at the smokehouse, but it was in the back of his truck."

"You told him?"

"I told him about the bear and you. I told him we were burying the bear together. So he said he'd feed the hogs for me today. But he was really mad about the bear being tied to the swing. He wanted to call Willy's and Brian's fathers, but I told him I'd get them back—in my own way. And I will, Beth. I promise."

"I wish I could, too."

"No, I have to do it alone—but it will be for both of us."

Digging the grave was hard work, and although it was raining, Beth took off her rain-coat. The gentle sprinkle of rain was cooling against her sweating skin; but soon she was hot again, and desperate to take a rest. Not wanting to be the first to suggest stopping, she kept on digging. Finally she noticed Danny leaning on his shovel, watching her.

"Want to take a rest?" he asked.

"I sure do!"

"Me, too. This is hard."

"How deep do you think we have to go?"

"I don't know. Three or four feet maybe."

Beth gasped. "Do you think we can?"

"Oh, sure."

Dropping her shovel, Beth said, "Wow, you've done lots more than me."

"That's only fair. If it wasn't for me, we wouldn't be burying the bear."

Beth sighed and sat down on the ground. Looking over at the bear, she said, more to herself than Danny, "I don't think I'll ever swing again."

Danny knelt down next to her, and pulling at her arm to get her attention he asked, "Why not?"

"Because—dead bears and swinging don't go together."

"Don't say that. I'll feel terrible if you didn't swing here anymore."

"It's not your fault. You didn't tie the bear on the swing."

"But it is my fault—it's my fault the bear's dead."

"Well, maybe I'll just come here and sit on the swing like you do."

"That's stupid."

"Why? You do it."

"I know, but that's different. I haven't used the swing for swinging for a long time."

"How come?"

Danny shrugged. "I don't know. Maybe I'm too old."

"Now *that's* stupid! I'll never be too old for swinging. I think you should try it again."

"Why should I—if you're not?"

Beth didn't have an answer for that, so she said, "You know something? I used to hate to see you sitting on the swing. It made me so mad. I'd think, 'Why is he just sitting there? It's so dumb!' But I don't think it's dumb anymore."

Danny smiled. "I used to get mad when you were on the swing, too. I thought the swing was only mine, and you didn't belong. But I don't feel that way anymore either. I think I'd really miss it if you didn't swing."

"Oh, Danny, I'm sorry. But swinging is a happy thing. . . ."

"But this is still a happy place, Beth. It's better than ever. I used to come here only when I was sad—maybe that's why I stopped swinging. But now the swing belongs to all of us: you, me, my father and even the bears. And that's not sad at all."

Beth thought for a moment and said, "Are you going to swing then?"

"Well, I don't know . . ."

"See, you don't really think it's a happy place!"

"I do. Honest. It's just that I'd feel silly swinging. I can't help it."

"What if we did it together? Remember when we were little and I'd sit on the swing and you'd stand up on it?"

"How did you remember that?"

"I don't know. I just did. Would you do that?"

Danny smiled. "Yeah, okay. I'll do that."

"Promise?"

Danny nodded. "And this time I'll keep it."

It took the rest of the morning to bury the bear. When they were finished, Beth dug some wildflowers from the field and planted them on the grave.

"Do you think they'll live?" she asked Danny.

"Maybe—if the rain keeps up," he said, sitting on the ground. "It's a nice grave anyway," he sighed, leaning on his arms, pressing them onto the smooth surface of the rock. He was tired, and it felt good to lie back until all he could see was the huge leafy branches of the oak tree.

Beth nodded, and walked over to the swing. She ran her fingers up and down the rough ropes, pushing them gently, making the swing sway slowly back and forth. The image of the bear cub came to her and for a moment she felt the terror again. Closing her eyes, she tried to blot out the memory. *It's still the same swing! I can get on it now, like always. . . . I could swing and swing forever if I wanted. I could. I could!* When she opened her eyes, the swing was motionless, waiting for her.

About the Author

Emily Hanlon lives in Yorktown Heights, New York, with her husband, her daughter Natasha and her son Nicky. She has spent many summers in the New England countryside she describes in *The Swing*.

Ms. Hanlon has written two picture books, and a novel for young adults, *It's Too Late for Sorry*.